'Don't ever th

help,' Marshal

low and husky.

'Oh, Marsh, but I have *problems* at the moment,' she answered, feeling the relief at letting the words spill out. 'It's not fair to you, roping you into my life...'

He had stiffened a little. She felt it as if they'd been pressed length to length, except that it was still just that one finger, stroking her hand with an erotic subtlety she'd never imagined before.

'It's not a question of being roped in, Aimee,' he said very carefully. 'If you want me in your life, I want to be there. Is this about Friday night? Are you having regrets?'

The question was too sudden, too unexpected...and, since her brother's news, too accurate. Friday night had been utterly fabulous in itself, but as each hour went by the timing seemed more and more of a disaster...

After living in the USA for nearly eight years, **Lilian Darcy** is back in her native Australia with her American historian husband and their four young children. More than ever, writing is a treat for her now, looked forward to and luxuriated in like a hot bath after a hard day. She likes to create modern heroes and heroines with good doses of zest and humour in their make-up, and relishes the opportunity that the Medical Romance™ series gives her for dealing with genuine, gripping drama in romance and in daily life. She finds research fascinating too—everything from attacking learned medical tomes to spending a day in a maternity ward.

Recent titles by the same author:

THE TRUTH ABOUT CHARLOTTE
WINNING HER BACK
THE MARRIAGE OF DR MARR

A NURSE IN CRISIS

BY

LILIAN DARCY

MILLS & BOON®

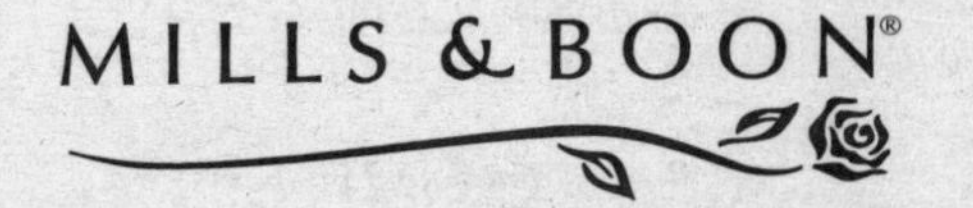

First published in Great Britain 2001
Harlequin Mills & Boon Limited,
Eton House, 18-24 Paradise Road, Richmond, Surrey TW9 1SR

ISBN 0 263 82650 3

Set in Times Roman 10½ on 12 pt.
03-0301-55116

Printed and bound in Spain
by Litografia Rosés, S.A., Barcelona

CHAPTER ONE

'Is IT serious, Dad?' Rebecca Irwin asked quietly.

Marshall met his daughter's intelligent blue-eyed regard across the reception desk of the GP surgery where they both worked. He rested his hands lightly on the papers there and took a moment to think about her question.

He hadn't expected it. Not right at this moment. The busy Sydney medical practice was quiet as its staff had left for the day. The computer hummed. Its screen-saver of furry yellow and black caterpillars crawling across a carpet of green leaves was now the most colourful thing in the waiting room.

Practice nurse Aimee Hilliard had been the last person to go, just a minute earlier, leaving only Marshall and his daughter. Marsh planned to phone Aimee tonight, and was quietly confident that she'd be pleased to hear his voice after hours. It wouldn't be the first time he'd made such a call, although he was taking things slowly…

'I don't know yet,' he answered Rebecca, as a pleasant and surprisingly physical warmth began to grow inside him. 'I'm starting to think it might be. I'd…' He hesitated, having to struggle to break down his natural reserve. 'I'd like it to be, actually.'

Rebecca gasped. 'Dad! What on earth—?'

She seemed appalled. Marshall felt his scalp tighten. She was staring at him, her mouth open and her eyes wide. In a matter of seconds, something had gone seriously wrong with this conversation.

'Let's get this clear,' she said carefully. 'I'm talking about Mrs Deutschkron's test results.'

'Mrs…?'

'There.' She gestured. 'Under your hand. The pathology reports, and hers is on top. I saw the name a few minutes ago when Bev handed them to you.'

'I haven't looked at them yet,' Marshall confessed, his scalp tightening even further. 'I hadn't even realised that hers was on top.'

'So what were you talking about?' Rebecca accused.

He was hot, now, as guilty and self-conscious as a child caught stealing lollies. 'Nothing important.'

But she wasn't buying it. She ticked his recent statements off on her fingers, one by one. 'You don't know yet. You're starting to think it might be. You'd like it to be.'

'I can see why you hoped it wasn't Mrs Deutschkron's test results,' he joked heartily.

'Dad… You meant Aimee, didn't you?'

'Yes.' He nodded briefly. 'Because I thought that you did.'

There was a rather long silence. 'Been wondering, actually,' Rebecca finally said.

She was standing by the door, running her fingers up and down the edges of the wooden Venetian blinds in an irritating manner. Marshall found it irritating, anyway. It was permissible to be irritated with grown-up, married and newly pregnant daughters who asked probing questions at the wrong moment.

Only, he remembered, she hadn't been asking about his feelings for Aimee Hilliard at all. He'd made the wrong assumption because of the direction in which his own thoughts had been moving, and as a result he now found himself having to talk about their relationship—which wasn't a word he liked these days because people always said it as if it had such a very significant capital R at the beginning of it—long before he was remotely ready to. So perhaps it was himself he was irritated at?

Yes, undoubtedly.

'Yet you haven't said anything,' Rebecca was now accusing him gently.

'Because there isn't anything to say,' he burst out, goaded beyond endurance.

Unfairly, of course. This was his own fault! Rashly, he ploughed on. That was the danger when you were reserved by inner nature and upbringing. Once you *did* open your mouth, you didn't know when to stop!

'Rebecca, please, don't put this under that mental microscope of yours!'

'Microscope?'

He ignored her. 'I wish the subject hadn't come up. I don't know what's happening. I don't know how she feels. I'm very rusty at this—'

'What did you mean, ''microscope''?' Ominous. Her voice wasn't quite steady.

'Bad word choice.'

'You think I—'

'No! *No*, Rebecca.'

'You know that all I care about is your—'

'Yes, yes, I *do* know that.' Marsh steadied himself, remembering too late that her pregnancy, which wasn't making her nauseous or even particularly fatigued, *was* making her rather fragile and volatile emotionally at the moment. Both he and Harry, his son-in-law, had been trying unsuccessfully to get her to slow down just a little.

'I'm sorry,' he apologised. 'This is all completely my fault. Can you accept that I'm not ready to talk about it yet, and that when I am—*if* I am, if there's anything concrete to say—you'll be the first to know?'

She nodded brightly. 'Of course, Dad.'

But the straight line of her mouth seconds later told him that she hadn't quite forgiven him for the microscope thing, or…perhaps more importantly…for the fact that something new and potentially important was going on in his life and he hadn't said a word.

'I'd better head off now,' she said, a little too abruptly. 'Harry was going to see a patient on his way home, and I told him I'd get there first and get dinner on. He'll be worried if I'm not in evidence.'

'Don't tire yourself out with elaborate cooking, Becca.'

'Frozen quiche and garlic bread, and a bag of salad greens,' she summarised dryly.

'Good girl!'

'See you tomorrow.'

A smile came and went too quickly, leaving a frown in its place, and then she'd gone. He could hear her youthful, energetic footsteps scraping on the half-dozen concrete steps that led down to the street. He listened until they faded.

She was too protective of him, that was the trouble. It had been that way for years, since her mother had died when Rebecca had been just fifteen years old. That was thirteen years ago now. Thirteen years…

For a long time, his grief for Joy had been overwhelming, and it had been Rebecca who'd held the family together, helped him to cater for ten-year-old Simon's needs, nurtured both of them in a hundred different ways.

Three years ago, he'd finally felt ready to consider marriage again, but his choice—made more as a matter of expediency than love, he could now see—had been disastrous. He'd proposed to his live-in housekeeper, who was ten years his junior, but, instead of politely turning him down, she'd acted as if it had been a case of sexual harassment and he'd been badly shaken by his misreading of her.

Rebecca had been furious on his behalf. At one point he'd had to talk her out of storming around to Tanya's new flat and demanding back the jewellery he'd given the woman.

'The jewellery isn't the issue, Rebecca!' he'd had to argue urgently. 'She's more than welcome to it as some sort of compensation if my behaviour was really so offensive.'

'Oh, of course it wasn't!'

'It's my own judgement that I'm doubting.'

'You should be doubting the mental state of the entire female sex over the age of thirty,' Rebecca had muttered darkly. '*I* am!'

Marshall sighed. He loved his daughter's passion, and her strong responses, and he knew that his son-in-law had fallen for those same qualities. There were times, however, when it might have been more...convenient...if Rebecca bore less of a resemblance to an angry lioness protecting the pride.

Absently, he looked down at the pathology reports still resting beneath his fingers. That was where this had all started a few minutes ago. Rebecca had wanted to know if Mrs Deutschkron's prognosis was serious. He picked up the sheet of paper and studied the details, and had the answer to his daughter's question a moment later—an answer which suddenly dwarfed his concern over Rebecca's attitude towards his blossoming new relationship with Aimee Hilliard.

It *was* serious. Far more serious than he'd thought it would be. Hilde Deutschkron had had exploratory surgery last Thursday for suspected cancer, but prior to that she'd seemed relatively fit and with few complaints about her symptoms. He'd had every expectation that any growth found by the surgeons would turn out to be localised and easy to deal with, effectively meaning a permanent cure.

Yet the results provided by Southshore Hospital's pathology department were unequivocal—cancer of the liver, with the primary tumour not located, which meant a spread of cancer throughout her system. No hope of a cure or of long-term survival. At best, the possibility of chemotherapy, which would prolong the patient's life for several months. Many people, in these circumstances, made the choice to have no treatment at all.

As yet, she wouldn't have been told any of this. Usually, it was the surgeon's job, but since he'd known this patient for such a long time he would do what he'd done once or twice before and phone the surgeon to suggest that he tell Mrs Deutschkron himself. It wasn't something any doctor looked forward to, but Marshall felt that it would come best from him.

And he couldn't shake it off, as he usually managed to. Hilde Deutschkron had been a patient at this practice since long before he'd started here, and that had been over twenty years ago. Her three children had been delivered by old Dr Rattigan, who was now retired. Her husband had been a patient here, too, until his death of heart failure six years ago.

Still, perhaps he might have shaken it off more easily if it hadn't come as such a surprise…

At home, an hour later, the big house where he now lived alone seemed too big, ridiculously big for one man. Simon was still studying in the United States. He'd met an American girl and they were now seriously involved. It seemed all too likely that he'd make his home there permanently.

Rebecca and Harry lived just a short drive away in Surry Hills, but even with the prospect of overnight visits from darling little grandchildren in the not too distant future—and, good heavens, it was difficult to adjust to the idea that he'd be a grandfather soon—he didn't need all this space. Should he sell and move somewhere smaller?

One of life's big chances, a decision to make, as Hilde Deutschkron would have to do soon, only her decision was much more grave.

He picked up the phone and dialled Aimee's number. What would she say if she knew that he could key in the eight digits off by heart now? Would she be pleased? Did she know his number, by any chance?

She answered on the first ring. Her voice was as cool and fluid and sweet as ever, but he hadn't expected to hear it quite so soon, and was startled into speaking more abruptly than he'd intended.

'Aimee? It's Marshall. I'm sorry, I was going to suggest we go out for a coffee later on. We talked about something like that on Sunday, didn't we? But I wouldn't be good company tonight, I'm afraid. The news on Hilde Deutschkron wasn't good...'

'Oh, no!'

He gave her the details, then added, 'And, well, as I said, I just wouldn't be good company.'

'That's fine. Of course. I understand completely. Perhaps you should go for a walk or a jog or something.'

'Good idea,' he agreed, and a few moments later he'd put down the phone.

'Or, Marshall, would it help if I—?' Aimee began.

Too late. She heard a click in her ear, and then the metallic trill of the dial tone. He'd hung up without hearing her belated addition. She took the receiver from her ear and just sat there in her silent house for several long minutes, trying to argue herself out of an absurd disappointment, trying to take herself back to the mood of the weekend they'd just spent together at the ski resort of Perisher in the Snowy Mountains.

Two couples had had to pull out of a trip some friends of Marshall's had planned, and he'd invited Aimee to join him in taking up the two spare rooms, already booked and paid for. They'd had a thoroughly wonderful time on the slopes and with Marshall's four friends. Simmering below this, as yet unacknowledged, had been a stirring of the senses she'd forgotten about, hadn't felt since…when? Her twenties? She already had a strong inkling about its importance.

Marshall had felt it, too. She was quite sure of that. They'd both sensed the unfurling of a physicality which had been dormant in each of them for a long time. But the six-hour journey back to Sydney after the weekend was over, in the four-wheel drive the six of them had rented, had broken the mood somewhat. Everyone had been tired, and the other two women, Penelope and Sandra, had been getting on each other's nerves.

At her home, Marshall had helped Aimee to carry in her luggage, saying to her quickly at the door, 'Can't stop. Geoff's on a short fuse.' He'd taken her hands between his and she'd loved the warm, engulfing feel of his touch. Then he'd said something very quick and sketchy about 'doing something together' very soon.

His swift, tender kiss had brushed her cheek and the corner of her mouth, lasting only a moment, yet more than twenty-four hours later it still seemed to tingle on her skin.

I'm falling in love with him, Aimee realised. I'm really, truly falling in love with him.

It felt wonderful, and at the same time very, very frightening. She was fifty and he was fifty-one. They both had grown-up children, including each of them a daughter who would soon make them grandparents for the first time. Perhaps, after all, it was good that he'd cried off tonight with that brief phone call. She really had to keep her feet on the ground about this!

For the next hour and a half, Aimee did just that. She did sensible things, like ironing blouses and teatowels, and cleaning the cupboard under the sink. She made herself a mushroom omelette for dinner, and washed the dishes immediately afterwards. She rang her son Thomas, who was doing three months of field research near Cairns, and her daughter Sarah, who was having a very difficult time with her first pregnancy, which had now reached the end of the second trimester.

Sarah fretted over the phone, 'My friend Louise says she never felt like this. And she thinks I look huge, but the ultrasound showed it's not twins.'

'When's your next appointment?' Aimee asked her daughter.

'Next week.'

'Write down all your concerns so you remember everything you want to ask the doctor. And if you're really worried, give him a call tomorrow and ask if he can see you sooner.'

It was sensible advice, received with thanks from Sarah.

Then Aimee spoiled it all by pouring herself a glass of white wine—only a small one—letting down her long hair, turning off all the lights except the stained-glass lamp on the end table and dancing with her eyes closed to a compilation tape that Sarah had made for her, featuring Elvis Presley, Roy Orbison and the Rolling Stones.

How old was fifty, anyway? Not old at all! Younger than Mick Jagger. And she'd just spent the weekend skiing, for heaven's sake!

Then the doorbell rang. It might, in fact, have been ringing for a while. There was no point at all in listening to the Rolling Stones unless you listened to them loud!

Half-empty wineglass in her hand and silver-white hair flowing down her back, she went to answer it, almost hoping that it would be grumpy Gordon Parker from across the street, complaining about the music. Her lounge-room window was open and it was possible that the sound carried that far, although there was a thick screening of trees and shrubs in the way.

Gordon was only a year or two older than she was, but he was always on about 'young people today', and she always felt highly defensive on behalf of Sarah and Thomas and her youngest son William, who weren't 'lazy and rude and undisciplined' at all.

Here I come, Gordon Parker, and I'm going to vigorously defend my right to listen to 'Paint It Black' in the privacy of my own home at eight o'clock in the evening, although I may agree to turn down the volume a notch or two!

She opened the door.

'Uh…' Marshall Irwin began awkwardly.

Aimee gasped, and it was probably fortunate that she didn't have any pockets in her old black cotton and Lycra leggings to stuff the wineglass into, slurp of Chardonnay included. 'Marshall! Come in…'

He looked achingly good, incredibly masculine and a lot better than Mick Jagger. He'd obviously been jogging, though he was only slightly out of breath. A dark blue T-shirt clung closely to a sinewy and nicely muscled frame. Loose black twill-weave running shorts showed off legs that were no strangers to exercise. They were brown, knotty, strong and roughened by dark hair. It was only two weeks until Sydney's well-known 'City to Surf' race, which he entered every year.

In the surgery, he usually wore glasses. Aimee liked the aura of experience and wisdom which the rectangular wire frames lent to his face. At the moment he wasn't wearing them and she could see his eyes, and it was starting to be a distinct possibility that she liked those even better than the glasses. They were blue, like the blue of willow-pattern china, steady and twinkling and…uncertain.

'Should I?' he said. 'You look as if you're…' He stopped.

Having a party? Oh, hell, this was embarrassing! Lonely widow, dancing her heart out in the dark. Secret women's business, indeed!

'I'm not,' Aimee said. 'At least, I *was*, but…'

'Sorry?'

'Please, come in!' She practically dragged him through the doorway by both hands, with the wineglass pressed between her fingers and his. 'I was…dancing, that's all.'

'Paint It Black' came to an end, and 'Pretty Woman' came on instead. Following her down the hallway, Marshall laughed. 'Dancing? All by yourself?'

'I know. It's—'

'Delightful! It's absolutely delightful, Aimee,' he repeated softly, and before she knew it he'd taken the wineglass from her hand and plonked it down on the sideboard, then whirled her to face him. He took her hands in his and began rocking along with her to the jaunty, driving beat. He was good at it, unselfconscious and naturally attuned to the rhythm. 'Do you do it often?'

'No!' she denied frantically, then added, opting for greater honesty, 'But I often feel that I should. When I *do* it, it's so nice. Not really a lonely feeling, dancing alone, because it's so exhilarating, and I usually phone Sarah or someone afterwards, and anyway William only left home at the beginning of the year…'

'Did he join in?'

'No, he laughed at me! But in a nice way. He thinks the

Rolling Stones are dreadfully old-fashioned. He likes Radiohead and Smashing Pumpkins and Powderfinger.'

'I'm impressed at the way you can reel off the names!'

The home-made tape came to an end, making the last few notes of the song wobble before they cut off, and the silence was too sudden. They both stood in the centre of the room like boats beached by a low tide.

'Ah-h-h!' Aimee said to break it, lifting her hair up onto her head to cool her neck. She was more breathless than Marshall had been after his jog.

'I had to come,' he said, his voice suddenly low and serious.

She looked up at him, alarmed.

'No,' he hastened to answer her. 'Nothing's happened. But when I told you I wouldn't be good company because of feeling low over Mrs Deutschkron's prognosis, I realised...I can already tell this isn't going to come out right!...that that was exactly why I should want to see you, and why I did want to see you. Damn!'

'Marshall?'

'I was right. It hardly sounds like a compliment, does it? That I was down, so I wanted to inflict it on you and added your house to the route of my evening jog. Oh, but, Aimee, I don't want to waste any more time on explanations! I don't! This is what I want...'

He pulled her into his arms slowly, with grace and care, as if it was something he hadn't done in a long time but had no doubts about the rightness of doing now.

Coming up against his chest, still breathless, Aimee had no doubts either. Her body and her heart were responding more strongly than she'd thought they had the power to do. Her heart was pounding, in fact, and her breathing was light and fluttery. They were both a little sweaty and damp, both dressed in soft clothing that clung intimately.

But before she had time to map the places their bodies touched with such electrifying effect, he was kissing her. Not the rather courteous, old-fashioned press of his lips to the corner of her mouth that he'd given her on Sunday evening, but a real, honest-to-goodness, hot, passionate smooch.

It felt…wonderful! And very quickly much more than a smooch. A… A… There wasn't a better word in any language she knew.

Oh, stop thinking about it, Aimee!

She did, and just gave herself to the endless moment instead. Slowly, his arms came fully around her, one hand resting against her hip at first, then sliding across to lazily trace the curve of her rear, still satisfactorily taut and shapely beneath the close-fitting leggings.

Marsh's other hand had crossed her back and kneaded her shoulder, and she had to arch and stretch her neck up to reach him with her own mouth, creating a strangely pleasant feeling that she'd topple backwards if he didn't have her so tightly and preciously enclosed in his arms.

His face was a little rough. His body was firm, and still hot from his run. His mouth was confident, as if now that he'd jumped in at the deep end he'd remembered that he was good at this.

And he *was* good at it! She hadn't realised until now that kissing was a talent like any other, and some people had that talent in spades.

He had a better talent than she did, too, of keeping track of a conversation, because when he finally broke away to ask, 'Do you understand that it's a compliment, Aimee?' she didn't have a clue what he was talking about. Of course a kiss was a compliment!

'I mean the fact that I needed to come,' he explained, after seeing her confused expression. 'It wasn't planned. I was jogging and I was heading in this direction, and it suddenly just wasn't possible not to come down your street and front up at your door and demand a cup of tea.'

'You haven't done that yet.'

'Can I do it now? This business of Mrs Deutschkron is still eating at me.'

'Oh, Marshall!' She reached up and pushed a stray lock of dark hair, thickly threaded with grey, back from his forehead. 'Of course it is! I'm so sorry, and here I am, dancing away like a maniac.'

She stroked her fingers down his jaw and neck, felt the beating of his blood briefly, then let them rest softly on his shoulder as she searched his face.

'Don't apologise,' he said. 'You hardly know her, and probably know nothing of her history.'

'No, I don't.'

He opened his mouth as if to launch into a story, then shook his head. 'We won't talk about it tonight. That's not why I came. I really just wanted…' he paused, then looked straight down into her eyes '…to be with you, Aimee.'

'I'm glad,' she managed breathlessly. 'Come through, and I'll make the tea.'

The mood had changed, but it was just as pleasant. They sat at the big kitchen table, talked about all sorts of things and drank their tea, warming their legs and hands in front of an old-fashioned electric fire.

It was the kind, at least fifty years old, that was shaped like a fireplace and had fake coals lit from beneath to make them 'glow', and was so ugly and silly that it had acquired the status of an antique by this time, and Aimee was perversely fond of it. It had once belonged to her grandmother. She liked it for practical reasons, too. A July night in Sydney could be chilly.

Marshall seemed to appreciate it. He stuck his bare legs

out until they were so close to the heat that they practically sizzled, and when he finally looked at his watch and took note of the time his jaw dropped. 'It can't be ten!'

'I know,' she agreed. 'But it is. I'll drive you home.'

'No…'

'Yes. Please.'

'I won't be annoying and argue the point,' he conceded. 'A ride home does sound a lot more pleasant than a jog, now that my legs are so warm and relaxed.'

They went out through the lounge room side by side, and there wasn't quite enough room as they passed the sideboard. He bumped it, and the glasses and china inside it rattled.

So did the half-empty wineglass she'd put down on the top of it two hours ago.

'Oops.' He reached a hand out to steady the glass and noticed the wine still sloshing inside. There was a tiny pause, then he said lightly, 'You never finished it.'

'It doesn't matter,' she answered him. But it came out just a little too hastily, and then she only made it worse by adding self-consciously, 'I don't often drink alone.'

'Oh, no, I wasn't suggesting…' He didn't finish the sentence, and there was a tinge of awkwardness in the atmosphere.

Why did I say that? Aimee scolded herself inwardly. I *don't* often drink alone, but saying it only made it sound as if I did.

The moment passed as she reached the front door and opened it to let in a draught of chilly air.

'Brr!' Marshall said. 'Definitely too cold for running shorts!'

They talked about the weather for the whole car journey to his place. Only five minutes between their two houses, so it wasn't so disastrous a subject, but Aimee still felt an odd discomfort and disappointment. Was she still smarting over that silly exchange about the wine?

Surely not! What was it, then? It had *something* to do with the wine.

Outside Marshall's gracious old house his kiss was brief and he didn't ask her in.

Driving home alone, Aimee probed at what she felt in the same way that she might have probed at a sore tooth with her tongue, and finally concluded in her mind. It's still early days. That's what rattled me about him noticing the wine. For a moment there, he did wonder, and it's early days in what's going on between us. We've both lived full lives before this.

She thought about her twenty-six year marriage to Alan. It had been a relatively happy one. She'd entered into it with too many stars in her eyes, of course, at the age of twenty. Then they'd weathered some disappointments, disagreements, coolnesses, ongoing differences in outlook that they'd never really addressed. That sort of thing changed a woman's perspective, influenced the person she became.

Neither of us comes without baggage, Aimee realised. We both have children. Previous marriages. Past grief. Complicated finances. It wouldn't take much, at this stage, to make the whole thing seem wrong, or just too hard.

Letting herself into her house, she saw that the 'on' light was still glowing on her sound system. She turned it off. No more dancing tonight. Time to go to bed.

CHAPTER TWO

'SORRY...I'm going to interfere, Dad,' Rebecca said.

'Go ahead,' Marshall invited.

He'd known this had been coming when she'd suggested they have lunch together, but he'd accepted her suggestion with an innocent face and had proposed the local Asian noodle house. Now Rebecca was toying with a plate of Pad Thai and making a very obvious effort to be calm and pleasant.

He waited as she gathered her thoughts, and wondered with a distant sort of curiosity about how he was going to react to what she had to say.

She was still struggling.

'It's about Aimee, isn't it?' he prompted helpfully.

'Yes.' She looked up. The noodles were still untouched. 'And it's not that I don't like her. You know that. She seems very nice and, of course, I've known her for longer than you have, since we met when we were both working at Southshore Health Centre.'

'But,' he supplied, still helpfully.

'Just...be careful. Perhaps you don't need me to say it. Probably you don't. You're an experienced, sensible man.'

'Thank you!'

'But I know how hard it can be when two people are working together. Harry and I nearly didn't reach the finish line a couple of times. Well, more than a couple! And it's not as if you're two carefree young lovers, who—'

'We're not lovers at all,' Marsh cut in deliberately, feeling a sudden need to assert himself. He wasn't a fool when it came to human relationships, and he was a private man. This was his business.

His daughter's uncomfortable shifting in her seat and sudden apparently starving attention to her noodles gave him a pinch of satisfaction. Rebecca had made her case, he now considered.

'I take your point, Rebecca,' he went on, making a conscious effort not to increase the gulf in understanding between them. 'And, of course, you're right. To a certain extent. Yes, we have more issues to consider at this point in our lives than a couple of twenty-year-olds. But I hope, as you say, that we have more good sense as well. I'm not sure what's happening yet, and I don't want office memos to be issued on the subject.'

'Of course not! I won't say a word. Even to Harry, if you don't want me to,' she promised extravagantly.

'I'd prefer that, yes, at this stage.' He nodded, and saw her eyes widen a little.

She hadn't expected him to take her up on that over-enthusiastic offer to keep a secret from her own husband, but he really didn't want it gossiped about for the moment, not even between husband and wife, and if that didn't convince her that he was being appropriately cautious, what would?

Everyone in the practice knew that they had been away for the weekend recently, of course, but he'd presented the event as what it essentially had been—a group of friends enjoying two days of winter sports, not a romantic interlude.

'You know I'm only saying this because I care about you, Dad,' Rebecca said, her voice suddenly husky with tenderness.

And he did know it, too. As well, he was guiltily aware that he'd once interfered in her relationship with Harry for exactly the same reason, and the result might have been disastrous on that occasion if Harry hadn't completely ignored his sage advice.

'Shall we change the subject?' he offered, and she greeted the suggestion with relief.

Marshall wondered later, as they returned to the surgery together, if she realised how relentlessly her words were laying siege to his inner equilibrium. In many ways he was as wary as his daughter about this new thing that had so unexpectedly entered his life. Rebecca had no reason to accuse him of not being careful.

If dwelling on things, and replaying conversations—and silences—over and over in one's mind were signs of being careful, then he was being positively obsessive. That stupid business of Aimee's wineglass the other night, for example. He could have kicked himself for that unforgivable moment of hesitation.

He could tell she was afraid he suspected her of being a secret drinker, and he didn't. She'd given him no reason to. Not at the snowfields or at work here in Sydney. Not during the three times they'd been out together. So why that moment of suspicion, flashing through his mind, that he hadn't managed to hide?

'Because I'm a doctor, I suppose,' he concluded, muttering to himself. 'I've had patients who did drink, when sometimes it was the last thing you'd suspect.'

Like fifty-eight-year-old Joan Allyson, who was first on his list this afternoon.

'How are you, Joan?' he greeted her, as she sat down in the chair opposite his desk.

'Fighting fit, I hope,' she answered, and she looked it. Short grey hair, trim, energetic figure, dangling earrings of a pretty red to match her red trouser suit. She had come straight from work, and was due back there after her appointment. 'I'm just here for my annual check-up.'

She'd been very good about such things for the past seven years, but it hadn't always been that way. She'd started drinking heavily about fifteen years ago, after a painful divorce, but she'd hidden it so carefully at first that no one had suspected. Not her grown-up children. Not her colleagues at the insurance company where she'd worked. Not even her family doctor!

Until she'd turned up one day with gout, indicated by her symptoms of pain and confirmed by the test Marshall had done, revealing high uric acid levels. At that point he'd suspected very strongly, but his questions on the issue had brought only flat denial.

After that, it had got worse and everyone knew. Her two children had each come to see him in turn to ask if there was anything they or he could do. Without her willingness to admit to a problem, of course, there hadn't been. Her health had deteriorated. There had been more severe episodes of gout, and treatment for venereal disease. She'd lost her job.

Finally, and he still wasn't sure what the trigger had been, although he suspected another one-night stand which had turned bad, she'd come to him of her own volition and had asked for help. She'd heard of a drug called Antabuse, which caused any alcohol intake to create strong feelings of nausea, and she'd been keen to try it. He'd prescribed it for her, but had also urged her to join Alcoholics Anonymous.

Since then, she hadn't looked back. Now, seven years since her last drink, she had a well-paid and satisfying job in the administration of the Sydney Opera House, her health was good and on this visit she had some news as well.

'I'm particularly hoping everything's all right today,' she said, 'because I'm getting married in six weeks.'

'Oh, Joan, that's marvellous!' Marshall said, and meant it. 'Congratulations!'

She beamed, and the warmth in the room was palpable. Marshall was honest enough to admit to himself that if it hadn't been for the advent of Aimee in his life, he wouldn't be basking quite so strongly in the reflected glow of Joan's obvious happiness. But, to be truthful, he did find it very encouraging that love could run smoothly on the far side of fifty!

'He's a violinist with the Sydney Symphony Orchestra,' Joan went on. 'And he's got an adventurous spirit. We're going to East Africa for our honeymoon. Will we need any vaccinations?'

'Yes, I'm sure you will, but I'll have to check the most up-to-date information,' he told her. 'Why don't you make an appointment for next week? I'll make sure I have what you need in stock. Meanwhile…'

He gave her a thorough check-up, including a pap smear and a good listen to her chest and heart. In a minute, Aimee would take some blood to be tested for lipids, and he finished his own part of the check-up with, 'How long since you had a mammogram—do you remember?'

She made a face. 'I was afraid you'd say that.'

'I can easily check it in your file.'

'No, I know perfectly well I'm due for one.'

'The mammography screening unit at Southshore Health Centre would be the easiest place to go.'

'Will I have to wait? I'd really like to have it over with before the wedding.'

'That shouldn't be a problem. But do you really hate it so much? It doesn't hurt very badly, does it?'

'Spoken like a man,' she teased. 'Yes, it does hurt a fair

bit, especially if you have largish breasts, on top of which it's not remotely dignified. Oh, I'll be glad I've done it, but it's not exactly something to look forward to.'

'I suppose not,' he agreed on a laugh. 'Rest assured, though, we males of the species have our own unique and painful medical indignities to endure!'

'True,' she conceded.

The rest of the afternoon's patients were routine, with some more interesting than others. After over twenty years in general practice, Marshall was used to the rhythm and flow of the work. If he'd been a composer, he could have written a piece of music to express it.

Intertwining pastoral melodies for all those rather benign things like children's ear infections, annual flu shots, blood-pressure measurements. The interest lay in the way he got to know his patients year by year as he watched the wheels of their lives slowly turn. Patients he'd known as children were now grown up and married with families of their own. Patients he'd first seen in their fifties were now making decisions about retirement homes.

Then there would be plodding underbeat for the cases that few doctors could find interesting. Patients who came once to have a cut stitched or an ear syringed and were never seen again. People who needed a medical examination for work or insurance purposes and had phoned this practice purely because it was on a list of approved ones in the area.

There would be a burst of joyful song for wanted pregnancies, good test results, serious illnesses cured. And, finally, there'd be the keening of violins for the patients that broke your heart.

Like Hilde Deutschkron. He'd spoken to her surgeon on Tuesday morning. Today was Thursday, and she'd been discharged from the hospital this morning as planned.

After his last office appointment for the day, Marshall drove to her small house several streets back from the beach at Bondi and knocked at the front door.

Mrs Deutschkron's daughter, Marianne, answered. She was an attractive dark-haired woman of about thirty-eight, and Marshall had seen her a few times years ago for minor illnesses when she'd still been living at home. Since then, she'd led an interesting life as a journalist, with several stints of living and working overseas. She wasn't married, and he was pleased to find that she'd taken time off work to help her mother convalesce. Mrs Deutschkron's two sons lived in Melbourne and he knew she got lonely at times.

'How are you, Marianne?' he said. 'I don't suppose you remember me…'

'Of course I do, Dr Irwin!' she said with a confident smile. 'How could I forget the man who came at me with a cauterising thingy that time I had that strange lump on my little finger that kept bleeding if I bumped it?'

'That's right,' he said. 'I'd forgotten all about that. We never really decided what it was, did we? The cauterising didn't work, I remember, and it came back. You had to have it cut out under local anaesthetic at Southshore Hospital.'

'I'm amazed you remember!'

'Only because it stumped me, and the doctors at Southshore, too. Did it ever come back after the surgery?'

'No, but I still have the scar.' She stuck her little finger up in the air, then lowered her voice and said, 'Come through. Mum's on the couch, though I think she should really be in bed. She's not feeling very good, and she's anxious to hear your report. Do you have all the results or whatever everyone was waiting for?'

'Yes, I do,' he said, following her down the rather dark

corridor. 'Uh, would it be too much trouble to ask for some tea?'

'Of course not. Straight away?'

'If you don't mind.'

Marianne nodded, and he saw that she understood. There was a brief flare of well-schooled alarm in her eyes. Marshall didn't really need tea, but he wanted to break the news to Mrs Deutschkron alone. He had no doubt she'd need her daughter later, but for those first few moments…

'Hello, Mrs Deutschkron!' he said, coming into the thickly decorated sitting-room. There was a floral lounge suite, photos and knick-knacks everywhere, two shelves of books, vases of silk flowers, and all of it immaculately dust-free. 'Marianne says you're not feeling too good?'

'Would you be?' she retorted weakly. She'd lost weight since he'd last seen her, just before the surgery, and it was starting to show in the loose fit of her clothing, though there had been a time, long before he'd known her, when she had been far, far thinner than this.

'You have some news for me, don't you?' It came out abruptly, coloured by the accent she hadn't lost even after more than fifty years away from her native Germany.

'Yes, I do.' He sat down in the armchair at right angles to the couch where she lay, her legs and torso covered in a mohair blanket. 'And not good news, I'm afraid.'

He knew she wouldn't appreciate prevarication. Even his tiny pause now was pounced on.

'Don't keep me in suspense, then!'

'There was cancer throughout your liver, and the surgeon was unable to locate the primary tumour. That means the cancer didn't originate in the liver. It has metastasised from a primary tumour elsewhere. Chemotherapy is an option for you, but it won't be a cure. It'll give you several more months, that's all. I'm sorry, Hilde, there's no easy way to say this.'

She'd taken a sharp in-breath as she'd understood the truth, and now she was nodding slowly. 'I'm dying, then.'

'Yes. It was a surprise. Had you been feeling more discomfort and pain than you told me about?'

'Ach! Pain!' she said dismissively. 'It's relative, isn't it? Where's Marianne? You sent her off to the kitchen, didn't you?'

'Yes, I did.'

'Thank you...'

They could both hear the rattle of bone china teacups on their matching saucers, and the sound of cupboard doors opening and shutting. 'Shall I call her in?' Marshall asked.

'No, let her wait for the kettle. I'll just...digest this.'

She sat in silence, thinking, and he waited, wondering whether to reach out and touch her hand. He decided after a moment that she wouldn't appreciate it, and stayed where he was.

Then she looked up. 'So, may I articulate this situation more precisely?'

'Of course, Hilde. Any questions, anything at all...'

'I'm seventy-two years old. I am dying from a cancer that has spread throughout my body. I can choose to let death come soon... How soon?'

'A few months,' he offered. 'Three or four, perhaps. It's very hard to say.'

'Or, by having a course of chemotherapy, I can live longer. Again, how much longer?'

'Three or four months more. I'm sorry, it's so hard to be specific. Everyone is different.'

'The chemotherapy will make me sick.'

'Probably.'

'And I'll lose my hair.' She touched the grey knot on top of her head.

'No, actually, you won't with this particular treatment.'

'Ah, a plus! Not that my hair is so magnificent!'

They both smiled a little. In the kitchen, the kettle began to sing. Mrs Deutschkron was silent.

'I've fought death before, you know,' she said suddenly. 'In Berlin, in the war, and in a place in Poland which I won't name!'

'I know you have.' He nodded. Of her entire extended family, she had been the only survivor of those nightmare years in Europe, and had come to Australia in 1947, aged twenty.

'But do I wish to fight it now? That is what I have to decide.'

Marianne came in with teacups, cosy-covered pot, milk, sugar and a plate of biscuits on a tray.

'What is it you have to decide, Mum?' she said.

When she heard, she burst into tears.

'She's urging her mother to have the treatment, but I'm not sure if that's best,' Marshall told Aimee. 'As you know, a lot of people react very badly to it. I hope Mrs Deutschkron feels able to make her own decision.'

'Her daughter cares about her?'

'Oh, very much. Which can make people selfish sometimes.'

'And the reverse. It can make people sacrifice their own desires and needs.'

'I have a sense that Mrs Deutschkron is going to think about it all very carefully before she makes up her mind. I've told her there's no rush. She needs to be healed from the surgery first. I'll wait a few weeks before I press her for a decision.'

'Yes, it's not something to rush, is it?'

They stood in silence for a moment, and Aimee felt the sleeve of Marshall's shirt warm against her bare arm. Although it was only the end of July, this Friday afternoon was sunny and mild, and she'd taken off her light jacket to reveal a black-and-white-striped knit shirt beneath. Zebra stripes. Appropriate for a visit to the zoo.

She hadn't understood, at first, when Marshall had suggested the idea. 'Since we're both off work on Friday afternoon, can I extend the dinner plan we've already made to include something else?' he'd said to her the previous day, catching her during a quiet moment in the corridor at the practice.

'That would be lovely,' she'd answered, having had to conceal just how much her heart had jumped with pleasure at the thought of spending more time with him. Quite shamelessly, she hadn't cared a bit what it was! An invitation to help him fill out his tax return? Delightful! A trip to the local garage to get the spare tyre fixed? A dream come true!

'I'd like to introduce you to Felix, you see.'

'Felix...' she'd echoed blankly. Who was that? Not his son, she knew. A brother? Evidently someone important...

But he'd grinned. 'Can't quite call him a friend. More of a protégée.'

'Ah.' She'd nodded seriously. A young medical student from a disadvantaged background, perhaps? But that didn't seem...

'I sponsor him. The name's not official, by the way. He's a black-necked stork at the Taronga Park Zoo. I've told him all about you and he's dying to look you over.'

'Oh, Marshall!'

Another grin, quite shameless.

'You really had me going there!'

'I know, but I'm very fond of the zoo. I'm a ''zoo friend'', and a diamond sponsor member. There's a collared peccary at the Western Plains Zoo with whom I have a special relationship as well.'

'And what's his name?' Aimee had asked, entering into the spirit of the thing.

'Hers. Calliope.'

'Felix and Calliope,' she said. 'The sort of names one considers calling one's children, and then doesn't dare, in suburban Australia, in case they're teased at school.'

'Exactly. Will you come?'

'I'd love to!'

So here they were, watching Felix and the other birds disporting themselves in the still, greenish, dust-covered water of this pond from their viewpoint on the boardwalk bridge that crossed over it. Felix certainly was a handsome fellow, with his long, salmon-pink legs, lethally curved black bill and green and purple iridescent neck and head. He had a white breast with a black back and belly, and when he spread his wings the big white feathers spread like fingers.

Taronga Park had to be one of the world's most beautiful zoos. Situated on land that sloped down towards the harbour, amidst a jungle of semi-tropical greenery, it had magnificent views from numerous vantage points, taking in the blue-green water and the constant plying to and fro of sailboats and ferries and ships, the black fretwork of the Harbour Bridge in the distance, and that other landmark which could have been a clipper ship in full rig but was, in fact, the Opera House.

'Almost criminal to leave the place to tourists,' Marshall commented as they crossed the boardwalk bridge and set off in the direction of the reptiles.

'It is, isn't it?' Aimee agreed. 'I haven't been here since

the children were preteens, and that's too long. Why are locals, in every part of the world, so blasé about the treats that their home town has to offer?'

'Inertia?' he suggested. 'Our senses and our imaginations get dulled by the daily routine. It's something I decided to teach myself after Joy's death… Oh, it's trite when you say it, but true on a level I didn't understand before I'd felt that grief. To strive to *live* each day, not merely exist. I brought some cousins from England here several years ago, and that's when I decided to get involved with the place.'

'Zoos need people like you,' she told him. 'I'm afraid I…do coast a bit perhaps. I have my garden, the children and now my work. But nothing else that I'm really energetic about, or committed to.'

'Nonsense, Aimee!' he said. 'You seem like one of the most alive people I know, not openly passionate about things like my daughter is, bless her, but game for whatever comes your way—like the skiing on the weekend. And you're thoughtful, perceptive—'

'Stop!' she protested. 'I wasn't fishing for that.'

'I know you weren't,' he said, a little gruffly, 'but I wanted to say it all the same.'

He looked across at her, a fresh sea breeze ruffling his hair for a moment before they passed into the interior display of reptiles, and she couldn't miss the heat in his expression. It made her insides dissolve like melting chocolate to realise that he was happy to show what he felt this way.

She let her own gaze linger on features that were starting to be so familiar and important. His blue eyes with the laugh lines at their corners. A straight line of a mouth that could curve to express so many subtle nuances of humour and opinion—quizzical interest, amused irony, studious patience.

And then he slipped his hand into hers and all she could

think about was that, the smooth touch of his palm engulfing her fingers, his shoulder nudging hers as they walked and the dry, pleasant timbre of his English voice.

They stayed at the zoo for nearly three hours, then he dropped her home to change, picking her up again an hour and a half later to take her to dinner. They'd arranged this meal at one of Sydney's most exclusive harbour-side restaurants more than three weeks ago, before Marshall had even suggested the skiing trip that had taken place last weekend.

Thinking back to the cautious way Marshall had explained, back at the beginning of the month, that the booking for the restaurant needed to be made well in advance for a Friday night, Aimee marvelled at how far their connection to each other had advanced in so short a time.

Then he hadn't been certain that they'd both still want an intimate dinner like this three weeks into the future. Now she felt a rich wash of pleasure just at being with him like this, loving the way he shared his feelings about the working week…and even the way he brazenly stole one of her oysters fifteen minutes later when their appetisers arrived. He would never have done that—and he wouldn't have grinned like a little boy as he'd done it—if they hadn't felt so right in each other's company.

It was a magic, sophisticated evening after the frivolity of their trip to the zoo. He wore grey—a dark grey suit, with a steel-grey shirt and tie, simply cut but with a quiet distinction of style that could only have come from one of Sydney's best men's outfitters.

She loved dressing up for him, matching his subtle elegance, wearing clingy, simply cut black, with her pale, silvery hair folded and pinned high on her head. She'd had to ransack her jewellery box for things she hadn't needed—or bothered…to wear for years. A necklace of silver and garnets which had belonged to her grandmother. Matching earrings. A bracelet engraved with a subtle, filigree design.

Over dessert and the last of the white wine, Marsh started playing with the bracelet, rolling it around her wrist with his finger so that she could feel the warmth of his skin against hers. It made her want more—more of his touch and his company, more of his conversation, which had all the seasoning of a mature man's knowledge and experience, yet none of the rigidity and complacency that some of her women friends complained of in their husbands and which Alan had started to display when he'd reached his late fifties.

Perhaps it was because Marshall had been widowed while still in his thirties. His two children had been his closest companions, closest to his heart, and he'd retained their vigour and freshness of outlook. He'd said something about that time in his life that afternoon—that it had been Joy's death which had taught him how to live.

His own thoughts had been travelling along a sober path as well.

'I've been thinking about what you said earlier today, at the zoo, about sacrifice,' he said, as their dessert plates were taken away, and she was pleased that he'd remembered their conversation so clearly and had thought it important enough to mull over.

'Yes?'

'You're right,' he told her. 'Looking back on my experience, sacrifice is more common when there's a change or a crisis involving people who care about each other. Knowing how her daughter feels, I wonder if Mrs Deutschkron will do what she thinks is best for herself, or what she thinks is best for Marianne.'

'You won't try to influence how she decides?'

'I hope not. It's hard. A doctor has to try to present the

options in a neutral, factual way so that it truly is the patient's decision. But if you do know your own opinion, it's sometimes almost impossible not to let that colour the way you talk about it.'

'And do you have an opinion in this case?'

Marshall sighed, and let his fingers trail down to rest across the back of her hand. She felt his heat begin to rise all the way up her arm. 'I'd be inclined to say, ''Leave it, and enjoy the time you have left'', but if she decides otherwise, I'll do everything I can to help her retain her quality of life during the treatment and afterwards, as will her oncologist, of course.'

'It sounds as if that's all you *can* do.'

'Yes, and I'm sorry we're still taking about it.'

'Not still. Again. We haven't talked about it for hours. And it's fine, Marsh. I'd hate to think you'd edit your conversation out of a desire to spare me,' she told him, meaning it.

'Making sacrifices of your own?' he teased. 'Putting up with me to that extent?'

'It's a thankless job, but someone has to do it!'

They both laughed.

Outside her house, half an hour later, he left the engine of his car running. Listening to its subtle purr, Aimee began to shape her mouth into a polite thank you, before an equally polite goodnight. Then she rebelled. That wasn't what she wanted. Not tonight, after the deepening connection created by the time they'd spent together. It wasn't even ten o'clock yet, and the weekend lay ahead.

'Turn it off, Marsh, please,' she begged him boldly. 'I'd like you to come in.'

'Would you?' A light flared in his eyes, and there was a little catch in his voice.

'We didn't have coffee at the restaurant,' she hedged,

her courage already slipping. 'We could talk a bit more, and—'

But he hadn't heard this last part. The engine was off. He'd opened his door. He was through it, out of the car and bouncing onto his feet. Oh, heavens! Her heart started to beat faster and she was battling to suppress her grin of relief and pleasure. Courage? If she didn't have it, he certainly did!

He'd wanted her to say that! Wanted it rather badly, if the swiftness of his response was any guide. And he didn't care that she knew it.

Aimee was laughing as she got out, coming round the front of his streamlined car. And she was planning to say something clever and tender, like there was no point in his getting to the front door first because *she* had the key, but he didn't give her the chance to say anything at all.

Instead, he turned suddenly and she cannoned into his mouth, then felt his arms wrapping her in a hug like a huge, friendly bear. She'd never known a kiss to get off to such a flying start, and for the first half-minute of it she was still laughing. Laughing against his lips, then with her head thrown back as he made a trail of moist fire from the edge of her jaw to the top of her collar-bone.

'What's funny?' he growled, pulling off his glasses and sticking them heedlessly in his hip pocket, then glowering at her.

'You're so good at this!'

'I should hope so,' he growled again, and came back to her mouth for more. Much more. A hungry devouring of her that was so decisive it made her limbs as weak as water. 'Admittedly, I haven't been practising lately, but—'

She laughed again, and he frowned. 'No, seriously, Aimee, is there something that—?'

'Seriously,' she whispered, 'I think this is what's known

as being swept off my feet, Marshall. One minute I'm walking around your car in a very sedate manner, and the next I'm…' She took in a slightly ragged breath, unable to describe it. 'And it's fabulous.'

'Oh, it is, isn't it?' he said. 'Aimee, I don't think that…well, that my feet are any closer to the ground than yours are.'

Marshall laughed, a rich, full sound from deep in his diaphragm, and shook his head, his brow slightly furrowed in bemusement as if he couldn't quite believe that those words of confession had come from his own mouth. Then his lips claimed hers hungrily and fiercely once more, and his hands cupped the curve of her behind, sliding the silky fabric of her dress upwards.

'Shall we go in?' she said breathlessly.

'If you can hold the key steady enough to get it into the lock,' he answered. 'I'm not sure that I could!'

She managed it, with his hand still roaming her back and his impatience and eagerness sounding clearly in the rhythm of his breathing. As soon as they were both through the front door, he kicked it shut behind him and engulfed her with his touch once more, turning her mouth into a swollen, tingling mass of nerve endings and her breasts into two aching buds and her insides to sweet, warm jelly.

'We talked about coffee,' she almost gasped at him. The words hardly made sense, barely escaped from her lips in recognisable form.

'I don't want it,' he said, still painting her mouth with heat and pressure. A moment later he apparently thought better of the shameless response. 'That is…'

He stopped and schooled his voice and his expression. Again, she almost laughed. It was the worst performance of upright social manners she'd ever seen!

'Yes,' he said, his voice burred with effort. 'Coffee. Of course. That's why you invited me in, isn't it?'

'It needn't be. It wasn't really. Actually, it was the furthest thing from my mind,' she said in a low voice, hearing her own words with a stab of shock.

It was impossible to pretend. Her meaning was obvious to both of them, and she hadn't stopped for a moment to think about what she was offering, and why.

Her body. Her bed. Why not? She was a grown, experienced woman, confident in her judgement of character and of her own feelings, and he was her male counterpart. There was no one to disapprove, no one to hurt, few physical risks.

She knew enough of him and his history to be certain that if he'd had a lover since his wife's death thirteen years ago—and somehow, she doubted he had—then it would have been a woman much like herself, careful in such matters, not someone who slept around.

'What are you saying, Aimee?' Marshall demanded softly.

He knew. Of course he did. But she understood that he wanted to make sure that she meant it, and she loved that chivalrous quality in him. He was old-fashioned enough to want to protect a woman from any regret she might feel after the event at having let her body dictate the pace.

But *she* was old-fashioned enough to blush at the idea of putting it into words. 'Don't make me say it,' she murmured, her eyes wide and honest. 'Just…just take it, Marshall.'

'I'd love to,' he said. 'Did you plan this?'

'No. No, not at all.'

Marshall saw the sudden doubt and questioning in her eyes at once, and understood the new feeling.

'Does that make it…less appealing to you?' she said to

him hesitantly. 'Would you have preferred me to—I mean, it's not as if we have to think about—'

'No.' He shook his head vigorously, his mind leaping ahead once again to understand her meaning. 'No, Aimee! Nothing could make you…this…less appealing. And the fact that it was an impulse on your part, and so strong…'

'Then isn't that enough?' she said. 'There's no reason in the world why this shouldn't happen, and every reason why it should. That's more than enough for me.'

'And for me,' he whispered, and kept on kissing her with an intensity that made both of them tremble, all the way along the corridor to her bedroom.

When they reached her bed, their need reined itself in a little, overtaken by 'first-night nerves' that he wasn't afraid to admit to.

'If you hear a squeaking sound in a moment, don't worry,' he said to her in a low voice, still holding her close. 'It'll only be the rust.'

She understood at once, and answered, 'I can hear it already, only it's coming from me. Marsh, I'm not—I've never—'

'Let's make some rules,' he suggested, lacing his fingers in the small of her back as he held her more loosely.

'Rules?'

'Let's not talk about the past, what we have and haven't done or felt, and how long since we've felt it.' He made a trail of tiny kisses from her forehead to her ear. 'Let's not put any pressure on ourselves or each other to succeed in some Hollywood version of this. We've succeeded already.' His lips brushed her mouth. 'Everything that happens from this minute on is just a bonus. That means we can take it at whatever pace we want to and that, whatever happens, it's safe.'

'Safe…' she echoed.

'I know what you're entrusting to me, Aimee. You know I'm going to look after it with all the care and tenderness it deserves. And what I'm entrusting with you is just as fragile.'

'Oh…yes. Thank you, Marsh. Thank you for saying it.'

She buried her face in the warmth of his neck for a moment, and heard a rumble of laughter from him, a mixture of relief and happiness and triumph, and she was so astonished and almost disbelieving that she'd managed to find a man like this that she had to pull away and simply look at him, laughing, too, at first until the magic between them made both their faces still.

In the silvery light that seeped into the room through the half-open curtains, his expression was serious and searching, and the lines of experience on his skin were softened so that the strong bone structure beneath was more apparent. The attraction between them was like a measurable force. It ought to have some sort of a scientific scale, she thought vaguely, like earthquakes did, and electricity. Volts or hector-pascals.

It seemed incredible that an attraction like this should be accompanied by such a sense of certainty and peace. On one level, she was a wild cauldron of feeling, but on another, at the centre of her being, there was calm, and those first-night nerves were ebbing by the minute.

Marshall had started to undress her now, with a tender reverence that had her breathing in little flutters as she held herself completely still so that she didn't miss so much as a moment of sensation. Wanting to touch and explore his skin, she slid his jacket from his shoulders and began to unfasten his steel-grey shirt, then loosened his tie and started on the shirt buttons.

When they stood naked together, he whispered, 'You're beautiful.'

She didn't try to deny it because she was too busy thinking the same about him. The texture of hair on skin, the taste of him, the smell of him…

They sat on the bed and he kissed her again, touched her in places that made her shudder, took his hands away when it became a little too intense and simply held her until she was ready to go further. Even when they were lying together, entwined beneath the sheets, and neither of them could breathe without making a jagged pattern of sound in the air, he was still able to pause, wait, let her become accustomed to the intimacy of it before they took another step.

Aimee hadn't known it could be like this, that each step could be so thoroughly savoured, like an endless banquet of tiny, exquisitely served courses. She hadn't known a man could possess such patience, pitted against such sensual need. She hadn't known that she could lie in his arms afterwards, sated and replete yet still wanting more.

It was the longest, slowest, sweetest and, in the end, most passionate night of love-making she'd ever had.

CHAPTER THREE

'AIMEE, it's Peter,' said her brother on the phone the next morning.

'Hello, Pete,' she said, pleased to hear his voice but self-conscious as well. Was it possible that she sounded like a woman who'd enjoyed a tumultuous first night of love-making with her new lover? Undoubtedly! She was still in her nightdress, and her hair was threading loose from the plait she'd hastily woven it into at about midnight last night. Midnight? Maybe later...

Long, silky hair could be a sensual tool. It could be swept teasingly across a man's chest or provide a cool waterfall for him to run his fingers through. It could also get in the way, hence the hasty plait, but Marshall had openly enjoyed the sight of her sitting up in bed, her torso bared as she efficiently braided the long strands in the soft glow of a single bedside lamp to show her what she was doing.

They hadn't slept until after the early hours, and her voice on the phone was now lazy and croaky with late sleep and sensual relaxation.

'Can I come round this morning? Are you free?' Peter wanted to know.

'Yes, I am, actually.'

Unfortunately, she could have added, but didn't. Marshall was on call this weekend, and had had to leave half an hour ago to see a patient at Burradoo Nursing Home who'd fallen and torn the fragile skin along her calf. They hadn't had time to eat breakfast together, although he'd taken her in his arms in that same imperious, joyous way he'd held her last night, and she'd responded in the same way.

'I really have to get home after I've seen Mrs Bacon,' he'd said, regret screwing up his face. 'I'm having the upstairs bathroom redone. The shower's been leaking and I haven't been able to use it for a month. I hate baths! There are two contractors coming round this morning to give me quotes for the job. Can I ring you later?'

'You don't need to ask, Marshall,' she'd told him.

And she'd known her eyes had been glowing as she'd said it. He hadn't seemed to mind. But now he'd gone, and the house felt solitary and just a tiny bit accusatory, too.

What did you do? the quiet rooms seemed to be saying. You didn't think about it very much, did you? And he's left his glasses behind…

'Or I could make it later,' she heard, and realised she'd missed the first half of Peter's sentence and possibly another sentence or two before that.

'Whenever you like,' she promised vaguely. 'It's fine, Peter.'

'I'll be straight round, then.'

'See you soon,' she answered automatically, and it only struck her after she'd put down the phone that Peter had sounded tense, agitated.

Or was that her guilty imagination?

She had no need to feel guilty, she told herself, as she put Marshall's glasses carefully in her bag and washed up the evidence of the early morning cup of tea they'd shared. No need at all. It hadn't been a one-night stand. It had been a beginning, important and meaningful.

Not knowing if Peter had eaten yet—it was only nine o'clock, she saw with some surprise—she began to get out some Saturday brunch things. He'd probably like eggs and bacon. Perhaps a crumpet. Coffee, of course.

Thinking about it, she was surprised he'd phoned so early on a weekend. It was unusual. Could something be wrong? Her breathing suddenly shallower, she ran through the possibilities in her mind. Their parents, Douglas and Dorothy Brent, had retired fifteen years ago to Queensland. Dad was eighty now, and Mum was seventy-six, but if there was bad news from them she wouldn't have heard it like this, with Pete ringing to ask with a cryptic edge to his voice if he could come round.

Similarly, if there'd been an accident to any member of his family—his wife Annette and their two school-age children, Cameron and Alethea—he'd have said it straight out and not wasted time making the traffic-filled journey from Strathfield.

Yet, focusing on their conversation properly at last instead of on her vividly physical memories of Marshall and the night they'd just shared, she became more and more convinced that this wasn't just a social visit.

At forty-five, Peter was five years her junior, and they were close. Good friends, she'd have said. She trusted him, loved him, respected him, and was very fond of his family. But they were both busy enough that casual Saturday morning visits to each other, just popping in for a chat and a cuppa, didn't happen.

He had something to tell her. She was sure of it now, and as she showered and dressed and finished the preparations for breakfast, she couldn't help feverishly and fruitlessly running through the possibilities.

When he arrived to find her rearranging the napkins on the table on the front terrace for the third time, she'd steeled herself to hear what she was now certain the news had to be. He and Annette were getting a divorce…

He hadn't wanted breakfast. She could tell from the way his face fell at the sight of it all laid out in the bright winter sunshine. His hand scraped back through his slightly thinning mid-brown hair. 'Oh…er…no. I haven't eaten, but… Not hungry, really.'

She wanted to mother him in a schoolteacherish kind of way, as she'd done over forty years ago when he'd been a toddler and she'd been a little girl who'd loved playing at doctors and nurses. 'Now you must sit down, you naughty boy, and have a proper breakfast!' she used to say.

Today, it seemed too inappropriate for a man of his maturity and she kept the words to herself, just quietly poured him a cup of coffee then said, more lightly than she felt, 'Spit it out, Pete, please. You're scaring me!'

His look was an almost comical blend of relief and agony, but then he gulped back what was almost a sob. Quickly, she bent and covered his hand with hers on the green linen tablecloth.

'Whatever it is, Peter, it's not the end of the world, and I'll help you in any way I can.'

'No. You don't know,' he said. He snatched his hand away and buried his face in his palms.

She saw his shuddering breath. It shook his shoulders. Then he firmed them and straightened. 'You're right. I just have to spit it out. It's your money,' he said, his tone almost unnaturally steady now. 'I invested it badly, as it's turned out, and I've lost it all.'

The strength drained from her legs and she let out a cry. She couldn't help it, though she felt a wash of remorse the moment she saw his stricken face. Still leaning on the circular table for support, she groped her way clumsily round to her chair and sat heavily, then for his sake managed a degree of brightness.

'I told you it wasn't the end of the world,' she said. Then she went on, more honestly, 'Oh, Pete, I thought you were going to tell me you and Annette were getting a divorce. I was all prepared to hold your hand, but—'

'No,' he groaned. 'If only it was something as easy as that!' Then he caught himself up and gave a bark of complicated laughter. She saw the shadows of fatigue and stress beneath his light blue eyes. 'Listen to me! That has to be the most ridiculous thing I've ever said!' he jeered at himself. 'The only good part about this is that Annette has been fabulous.'

'You mean…?'

'Yes, we're back to square one financially as well. No more early retirement for me, and Annette will have to go back to full-time work.'

'So you've known about this since…?'

'Yesterday. But we sat up practically all night, talking about it and looking at the numbers. I—I can't believe I got you into this mess, Aimee.'

'I don't quite understand,' she admitted. 'I thought you'd put it into some sort of fund, incredibly safe and conservative. You told me that was what you'd done. There's been nothing in the news about the collapse of any—'

He groaned again, gave another shuddering half-sob and told her how, yes, at first he'd placed Alan's life-insurance money into something very secure, but the percentage return had been so slow that he'd felt bad on her behalf and had become convinced that he could do far better for her elsewhere. He'd hated the fact that the payments weren't enough to keep her from having to go back to work.

Then he'd had a very sound tip about a new internet company. The usual forecasts. Not improbably rosy. Peter really wasn't a fool. The forecasts had struck the right balance between steadiness and a quick return. He'd planned to make a respectable profit over two or three years then re-invest the enlarged capital in something steady, giving her a much healthier monthly income.

Only, of course, there hadn't been a profit. Another more established company had beaten this one to claim this particular share of electronic pie, and the upstart enterprise was in receivership, with no assets and many, many debts.

It would have been easy to be angry with Pete if Aimee had been less fond of him, and if he'd been suffering any less than he obviously was, both on his own behalf and hers. Ultimately, she couldn't be angry for long, or let him see it in the moments when she was.

They talked about it all morning, looking at the figures and what they would mean.

What they meant came as a shock.

'I can't see any other choice, Aimee,' Peter said quietly. 'You'll have to sell the house. The council rates in this area are so high now and you've been planning to get a new roof put on and the back fence and driveway replaced. Those things really do need to be done, but you've no capital for it now.'

'No, I can see that.'

'And if there's any way you can increase your hours at work…'

She nodded, and hid her appalled reaction. 'That shouldn't be a problem. About the work hours. They've been wanting me to work full time. As for the house…' She painted on a smile. 'It's only a house.'

But it was the place where she'd brought up her children and lived through Alan's death. The old swing set was still in the back garden, and she'd been planning to spruce it up for Sarah's baby. The line of marks that Alan had drawn on the back of the laundry door to measure each child's height as they'd grown were still there, too.

And what Peter didn't know, of course, as he sketched

some new plans for her future, was that the house wasn't hers…

Alan had been fourteen years older than her, which had given him a maturity and dependability, at thirty-four, which she'd valued when she'd married him at twenty. On the other hand, she could now see, he'd never learned to treat her as an equal. Almost every decision in their marriage had been made by him alone, and by the time she'd matured enough herself to question this, the pattern had been set and had been impossible to change.

Alan had died four years ago, and she'd grieved with a degree of pain that had occasionally surprised her. She hadn't known that grief could be so physical! Her hair had turned completely silver in the course of just eighteen months.

Then she'd pulled herself together and got on with her life. For the first time she'd had to make her own decisions, although even when he'd been dying Alan had been unable to relinquish control and had made plans that affected her life on into the future. Since his attitude had come from his love for her and their children, Aimee hadn't questioned it.

He'd advised her to turn to Peter for help in handling her finances, which she'd done. He'd also told her, 'I've left the house to the children, in trust for you to live in for your lifetime or until you decide it should be sold.'

Since he'd inherited the house from his own parents, and Aimee's name had never been on the title deeds, it hadn't been an unfair decision.

'Keep that to yourself,' Alan had advised. 'They don't need to know yet that they'll have a nest egg. They're still too young to handle it sensibly.'

So she hadn't told the children, or Peter. Alan had always been a very caring father. He'd wanted to give the three children a security that couldn't be taken away, hence his decision to leave the house to them. It had, indeed, worked out as he'd wanted, in a sense that Alan could never have predicted, and each of the three of them would receive gratifying nest-eggs following the sale, but Aimee herself would be nearly penniless.

'You'll be able to buy a nice two-bedroom unit,' Peter enthused, 'and still have enough left to invest for your retirement—only don't trust it to me this time, Aimee,' he interrupted himself with a bitter groan.

Aimee just nodded. She wasn't going to tell Pete the truth about the house, or her children the truth about her investments, because she didn't want to give Pete any more pain and remorse, and because she knew her children would refuse to accept that the house and its proceeds were theirs if they realised this was all she had left.

She was on her own in this, in a way that she'd never been on her own in her life. She'd moved straight into this house from her parents' home on her marriage to Alan. She'd never had to support herself fully. But there was a first time for everything, and she was going to deal with it, she vowed inwardly.

Pete was staring at his fingernails, as if wondering which one to chew on. He'd bitten them as a child and hadn't broken the habit until his teens. Aimee's heart ached for him. This wasn't easy for him either.

'Pete, I'm glad I was wrong,' she teased him gently.

'Wrong?'

'About you and Annette getting a divorce. That would have been much, much worse.'

He looked up at her. He didn't speak, but his expression was a little less tortured at last and his nails were still intact.

'Thanks, Aimee,' he said at last. 'You've always been able to put things into perspective. 'I—I appreciate it...appreciate having you as a sister...more than I'll ever be able to say.'

What was it that people said? Things came in threes?

When Marshall phoned, just after lunch, Aimee fobbed him off for the rest of the weekend, trying to make her voice as breezy and normal as she could. 'I—I'm not going to be able to see you today or tomorrow after all, Marshall.'

'Is everything all right? You sound—'

Not normal at all. She could hear it, but couldn't control it, and seized on the first excuse that came to mind.

'Sarah's not feeling very well.' Which, at least, had the virtue of truth. 'This pregnancy is hitting her hard. I'm going to stay with her overnight. You left your glasses here,' she gabbled on, 'so I'll just drop them round on my way to her place.'

'Don't worry about them. Bring them into work on Monday. I have a spare pair.'

'Are you sure?'

'It's fine. Your daughter needs you.'

'Thanks, Marshall.'

With her mind still in turmoil over the sudden looming change in her circumstances, she knew it would be unfair to see him. Dangerous, even. She was aware of a gritty determination growing stronger within her every moment to deal with this all on her own. Marshall, of all people, must *not* know of it.

She hadn't fully analysed why she knew this so strongly, but it had something to do with maintaining her independence and the footing of equality on which their relationship had begun. She wasn't going to relinquish that. She wasn't going to set up the same pattern she and Alan had fallen into. She wasn't going to lean on anyone. Perhaps she should have fought Alan's insistence on her dependency years ago!

It was funny, really. So many of the old taboos had broken down. Everyone talked about sex and scandal and childhood adversity, but money troubles were still something you kept to yourself. Absolutely and definitely, she didn't want Marsh to know.

And she knew he would have seen in her manner that something was wrong, just as he'd understood the fact at once on the phone. But she didn't like lying to him about why she couldn't see him, so she did phone Sarah immediately afterwards and found that she'd been even more truthful than she'd known.

'I'm so glad you rang, Mum!' her twenty-eight-year-old daughter said. 'I feel dreadful. So bloated. No energy at all.'

'Shall I come over? I could even stay the night…'

'Yes, please!'

Aimee packed an overnight bag and watered some plants, thinking in the back of her mind that if she was going to be putting the house on the market in the next few weeks, the garden ought to be looking its best. She'd have to get some tradesmen in, too, to spruce the place up a bit. At Sarah's, an hour and a half later, she was greeted by Sarah's husband, Jason.

'She's asleep, thank goodness!'

'I'm starting to worry about her, Jason.' Aimee sighed, after she'd waved aside his offer of tea. 'I kept telling her she'd feel better soon, and she isn't. I really am worried.'

'So am I,' her son-in-law admitted. 'We've talked to a few people, and no one else seems to have been hit quite so hard, especially not in the second trimester. She's supposed to be feeling great. And at the supermarket this morning someone said Sarah looked like she ought to be heading straight for the hospital, she was so big, but she's got another three months to go.'

'Why hasn't she talked to her doctor about it?'

'She has, over the phone. He agrees she's having a hard time and maybe something's going on—too much amniotic fluid, he mentioned as a possibility, but we don't know what that means. Anyway, he doesn't think it's urgent. The ultrasound at twenty weeks was normal, so were the results of some blood test. Her blood pressure's normal, so are her urine testing strips, her glucose tolerance test, all that. She hasn't had any pain. He's going to see her on Monday morning, first thing. I kind of wanted her to push a bit harder with him, but she doesn't want to come across as a complainer or a troublemaker.'

He gave a shrug that wasn't nearly as offhand as it seemed. Aimee was very fond of her son-in-law. He and Sarah had been together as a couple since university, where they'd both studied law, and they'd married two years ago. Fair-haired, big-shouldered Jason was steady and caring, occasionally hot-tempered, very much in love with his wife and inclined to get stubborn and frustrated about anything he couldn't control.

'Do you think she's just being a complainer?' Aimee asked him.

He looked at her and said bluntly. 'No. I think there's something wrong. But what do I know? I'm just the dad-to-be. All anyone can expect of me is that I'll faint at the delivery.'

He stomped off into the garden to mow the lawn.

Oh, dear, Aimee thought as she felt another heartburn-inducing ingredient add itself to the rich mix already bubbling away inside her. First had come the syrupy afterglow and fluttery nerves she felt when she thought back on last night… Oh, it already seemed like so long ago! Then there was the gnawing worry about her financial security and now, worst of all perhaps, the growing intuition that Sarah's pregnancy wasn't proceeding according to plan.

Sarah woke an hour and a half later. Aimee had busied herself giving the kitchen a thorough clean, including scrubbing the terracotta-toned tiles behind the sink and emptying spilled crumbs from the cutlery drawer. Its grimy state was a tribute to Sarah's fatigue, as she was normally a fastidious housekeeper.

'Oh, Mum!' said a groggy voice in the kitchen doorway, just as Aimee was finishing. 'You didn't have to do this!'

'I wanted to,' Aimee said. 'I knew it must be getting to you.'

Sarah looked vast, and vastly uncomfortable. Her light brown hair was a mess that was long overdue for a stylish cut, and she burst into tears before she even made it across the room.

'Everything is getting to me,' she said. 'Don't I look a lot more than twenty-seven weeks pregnant to you?'

'Could the ultrasound be wrong? Is it twins after all? Occasionally, mistakes do get made.'

'Well, I could only see one set of everything. But what do I know?'

Unconsciously, she'd echoed Jason's irritable expression of helplessness, and Aimee felt just the same. With her nursing training, she knew that some women had a build-up of too much amniotic fluid, which could cause the symptoms that Sarah was having. This excess of fluid might signal a problem...or it might not. And she was certainly not enough of an expert to do more than agree with her son-in-law that something felt wrong.

All in all, it wasn't a great weekend, and once or twice Aimee was tempted to bail out, say goodbye and phone Marsh to suggest to him that they go sailing, or climb the

Harbour Bridge, or something equally daring and frivolous. But she held back the impulse with a foreboding certainty that she'd regret it deeply if she gave in to it, although she didn't quite understand the strength of this feeling.

Peter's news about her finances wasn't so disastrous, was it? Ultimately, money was so much less important than family. She could keep it to herself, put it out of her mind. It would be far worse if something was wrong with Sarah's pregnancy.

But comparisons like that weren't exactly cheering!

She didn't sleep well on Saturday night in the spare room at Sarah's and Jason's, which would soon—oh, please, God—become their baby's nursery. Memories of last night, and Marshall, kept threading their way through her body. The fresh smell of him, like sandalwood soap. The strength of his thighs. The patterns of hair on his arms and chest. His tenderness and his hunger. The way he breathed when he slept, his head still pillowed on her arm.

And when she wasn't thinking about Marshall, she was worrying about Sarah. She heard bare, female feet padding to the bathroom several times in the night, and once she heard her daughter's voice say, 'I feel like I can't breathe, Jason. I'm suffocating!'

The next day, she stayed on until late afternoon, helping Jason in the garden and tackling the bathroom, which Sarah also hadn't managed to clean properly for several weeks. The tile grouting was a model of rather frighteningly vigorous biodiversity which would only respond to detailed attention with an old toothbrush and an abrasive cleanser.

Downstairs, the fridge was packed with food and Sarah explained tiredly, 'I took a couple of days off work last week, and I had this stupid idea that I was going to cook some meals to freeze because the last thing I've felt like lately is making dinner when I get home, and Jason can't cook a pot of water. But, of course, I felt too rotten to do it, and now it's all going to go bad.'

So Aimee cooked as well, making three different dishes and dividing each of them into meal-sized portions so that there were two weeks' worth of dinners in the freezer to ease Sarah's load over the next month or so.

At home, finally, she again thought of phoning Marshall and actually got as far as putting her hand on the telephone and holding her finger over the first digit. What would he say if he knew that she had his number committed to memory? That was such a schoolgirlish thing to do, wasn't it?

And at the last moment she decided not to dial it after all, which didn't stop her from hoping that he'd ring her, but he didn't and the phone stayed silent.

Instead, she rang Pete. After having his news churn round and round in her brain for more than twenty-four hours, she had questions and she wanted answers. Not that she liked them when she got them!

'What about the dividends I've been getting? There's been money going into my account regularly, the same as before. Where has that come from?'

From Peter himself, it turned out. He'd been so confident in the ultimate success of the company that he'd tided her over financially until the real dividends came in, certain that they would eventually do so.

'But why didn't you tell me what you were doing? Why did you keep me in the dark like that?'

Because of Alan, Alan's attitude and what he'd said to Peter as he'd been dying, it turned out.

'He told me categorically not to bother you with money matters, to take the whole thing onto my own shoulders,' Pete said. 'He said you knew nothing about finances, and didn't want to learn, that he'd made all the money decisions during your marriage, and that was the way you'd want it to continue.'

That's not true! she wanted to say. I was never given a chance!

But it wouldn't have helped to say it, and perhaps it was her own fault for not insisting to Alan years ago that things change, so she held her tongue and offered only a murmured, 'Of course. I see,' in reply.

When the alarm went and Aimee had to get up to go to work the next morning, it was actually a relief.

'How's Sarah?' That was the first thing Marshall said to her, and she practically cried at the knowledge that she wasn't alone in this worry at least. There was someone else who cared. But she didn't want him to see the tears, and quickly blinked them back.

'Big and tired,' she answered him, more brightly than she felt. 'She sees her GP today. I hope he takes it seriously.'

'Then you do feel as if something might be wrong?'

They were standing just outside his office and he was leaning against the doorframe in the casual pose of a man who was fit and healthy and at ease with his body. She was close enough to feel his heat and to sense the pull between them. Close enough, too, to know that he wanted to touch her. One hand, held loosely at his side, was reaching out just far enough to brush her skirt, and she felt the swish of the soft cotton against her legs.

If she moved her own hand just a little, she could entwine her fingers with his. But something held her back. Was it simply that anyone—Rebecca, Harry, one of the receptionists, even a patient—might walk along this corridor at any time? Or was it more than that?

She felt overwhelmed, and it didn't seem right that so

many different emotional things were happening in her life all at once. Peter's news, Sarah's state. Marshall's new importance in her life.

And, of course, she didn't have time to worry about any of it now. Dr Gaines needed her to take a patient's blood, then Dr Jones had to remove some infected splinters from a six-year-old boy's foot and wanted her assistance. Little Michael Callahan needed a lot of soothing and distraction, and turned out to be out of date with his tetanus immunisation as well. Predictably, the news that he needed an injection came as the last straw.

Harry had three more patients waiting, and so it fell to Aimee to deal with a kicking, screaming child in an attempt to push the needle home without causing him a lot more pain than if he'd lain still.

When it was finally over she felt distinctly shaky and, with Michael's hysterical screams still ringing in her ears, she took refuge in the practice's small kitchen for a moment while she made a cup of tea. It was going to taste so good! Looking at her watch, she was somewhat shocked to find that it was still only half past nine.

'Is my watch right?' she asked receptionist Chrissie Dunhill in a helpless tone, when Chrissie approached from behind her, carrying an empty coffee-cup.

''Fraid so,' Chrissie said with a wry smile. She was a trim, practical woman in her mid-forties, with three teenage children and emphatic opinions on parenting. 'Everyone in the entire practice heard that child screaming. His mother looked grim on their way out.'

'I'm shaking,' Aimee admitted. 'How long did he yell before I managed to give him the needle?'

'I wasn't timing it, but it felt like a good ten minutes.'

'It felt like twice that long to me!'

Chrissie shuddered. 'I couldn't be a nurse,' she said, 'let

alone a doctor. I love working in a medical practice, but I don't know how all of you do it. Cutting and stitching and jabbing. Looking down people's throats and hearing all the details.'

'I love it, actually,' Aimee admitted. 'Hadn't realised, until I came back to it, how much I'd missed nursing all those years when I was at home, bringing up the children.'

'What is it, though? It can't be something perverse and twisted, because you're all such lovely people!'

'What is it?' Aimee echoed, and tried to put it into words. 'The importance of it, I suppose. The realness. I know that's not a word! The fact that every day I'm in touch with what really makes people tick, physically and emotionally. Something like that, anyway.'

She spread her hands, feeling the explanation had been inadequate, but Chrissie nodded as if it made sense.

'That's what Dr Irwin said to me recently, too,' she said. 'And it must definitely be true in his case, because if he didn't love it he could afford to retire tomorrow, go on a world cruise and still buy himself a Rolls-Royce when he got home!'

'Could he?' Aimee answered automatically, hearing the way her voice had pitched itself a little too high.

She knew nothing about Marshall's finances, and wasn't sure that she wanted to. Not yet. Not for a while. Not since Peter's news.

'Oh, heavens, yes!' Chrissie said, then she tapped the kitchen door neatly shut with her heel and lowered her voice. 'Maybe I shouldn't talk about it, but I've been dying to tell someone. I mean, of course Dr Harry and Dr Rebecca know already. Probably everyone does, more or less, so it's not as if I'm gossiping or anything. His father-in-law died earlier this year and left him a considerable amount of money. We all knew that—or I suppose perhaps you didn't, since it happened before you started—'

'No, I didn't have any idea.'

'But we didn't know how much, until I overheard him—Dr Irwin—on the phone a few weeks ago, talking to the father-in-law's solicitor in London.'

She detailed exactly why it wasn't her fault that she'd overheard, then finished with a guilty blush and an exclamation. 'Listen to me! I'll be honest. I could have made a noise so he'd realise I was still at the front desk, but I didn't! And you really are the first person I've told. It turns out to be over a million pounds! Isn't that incredible? That's at least two and a half million dollars. Perhaps closer to three.'

'Yes,' Aimee said weakly. 'You're right. It's a lot of money. I had no idea.'

'Obviously he's meant to keep it in trust for Rebecca and Simon. At least, that's what he said on the phone, but there's no actual provision for that in the will, apparently. I heard him say to the solicitor how touched he was that his father-in-law, whom he hadn't seen for quite a few years, trusted him enough to leave the money to him outright, in the knowledge that he would do the best for the children.'

'Yes, but, of course, anyone who knows Dr Irwin would realise that he'll do exactly that,' Aimee managed, reeling inwardly from Chrissie's well-meant gossip.

'Oops, there's Dr Gaines calling me,' Chrissie said. 'I expect she wants that printout I promised her...' Her voice trailed off into a mumbling reminder to herself about some administrative task that wasn't Aimee's concern. Then she opened the door and left the kitchen. 'Coming, Dr Gaines. I'm sorry.'

I wish she hadn't told me. That was Aimee's first thought after Chrissie had left.

She stood, leaning her lower back against the sink, sipping her hot mug of tea and almost burning her mouth and the palms of her hands, which were wrapped around the mug.

Last week it wouldn't have mattered. This week she knew already that it did. Till Peter's news on Saturday, and Chrissie's revelation just now, she'd assumed that she and Marshall were equals as they teetered on the brink of their new relationship, and she'd wanted that equality so badly.

She'd imagined him to be in more or less the same position as herself—comfortably situated, wealthier on paper than they were in lifestyle, thanks to their ownership—or, in her case, trusteeship—of a piece of real estate in Sydney's expensive eastern suburbs.

But, in fact, as she now knew, they weren't equals at all. The house in Woollahra felt like hers in many ways, but wasn't, and it was dangerous to forget that for a moment. She had no other assets, while Marshall was a millionaire, with the expectation that he'd manage his finances well and leave everything to his two children.

There were many people in this world who might now perceive her response to Marshall as a cold-blooded pursuit, an attempt to better herself by getting her hands on his money. The very thought made her profoundly uncomfortable, and although she knew that she wasn't in any sense a gold-digger, the disparity in their situations had her stomach churning, without her as yet being able to work out exactly why.

Rebecca Irwin appeared in the doorway at that moment.

'Oh, Aimee, there you are!' she said. 'I'm going to need you to help clean some grazes and suture a cut. It's a boy from the local school, who fell in the playground, and the teacher who brought him in seems very concerned. The mother is on her way.'

Aimee put down her half-empty mug and followed Rebecca, who was still chatting brightly and in a not particularly natural way. 'I'm sorry to have to tear you away from your tea. I know you had a tough time with Harry's patient.'

'I'm fine, now, Dr Irwin,' Aimee said.

Although married to fellow practice partner Harrison Jones, Rebecca had made the decision not to change her name on her marriage. She was a strong character, approaching each aspect of her life with enormous passion. Aimee liked her, but had become aware of a change in her manner over the past week, and understood the reason for it very well.

Rebecca knew, or suspected, that her father and his practice nurse were involved with each other, and she wasn't prepared to take the matter on trust. She was wary, protective of the status quo.

Protective of her inheritance? Aimee suddenly wondered. Quite a normal response, really. Not many people would stand happily by and watch a widowed parent get involved in a new relationship if that relationship threatened their own position in any way.

There was no time to dwell on it any further now.

'I'm not going to have a needle, am I?' said the seven-year-old boy who sat in Rebecca's office. He was accompanied by a teacher with a very serious face, holding an object wrapped up in a tissue and placed in a plastic bag. 'I heard that other boy crying just now. It must have hurt like anything!'

Rebecca flashed a look at Aimee, and just then the boy's mother, summoned from home by a phone call from the school, hurried in.

'Don't let them give me a needle, Mum,' Aaron Lloyd ordered his harried parent in a panicky voice. 'It's going to hurt, and I don't want it!'

There was another nerve-jangling battle to administer the local anaesthetic. A piece of broken glass, hidden in the bark mulch beneath the school's playground equipment, had cut deeply into the boy's knee, and it needed stitches. Despite having the area numbed, the boy still whimpered throughout the whole procedure.

This was followed by ten minutes of painstaking cleaning of the deep, grit-filled grazes that surrounded the cut so that they didn't heal over with pieces of dirt still inside. Finally Aimee was able to dress the whole area with gauze and tape.

'All finished,' she told him cheerfully, then noticed the teacher, Adam Perry, a young man of about twenty-five, clearing his throat nervously.

'Wait for us in the waiting room, mate,' he told Aaron. 'Have a look at the books and toys. I need to…uh…finish something with the doctor.'

Rebecca wasn't present at that moment. Aimee had taken Aaron to the smaller of the two treatment rooms in the practice, and it had been quite a squash with both Adam Perry and the boy's mother looking on. She wondered what more the young teacher needed to say.

'Dr Irwin is with another patient,' she started to say, then saw Rebecca usher the pregnant woman out. The latter waddled down the corridor just behind a limping Aaron.

'Was there something else?' Rebecca asked, coming across to the corridor to the treatment room. The boy's mother turned to follow Rebecca in.

'Yes.' Adam Perry nodded. He held up the bag he'd been so carefully holding. 'This.'

With the utmost care, he took the dirty object out of the

bag and they all saw at once what it was. A hypodermic syringe.

'Oh, my lord!' Mrs Lloyd hissed. She looked sick and faint. 'Did it—?'

'Yes.' The teacher nodded jerkily. 'It was hanging from his knee when he stood up. Sticking in, but not very far. He was crying. He'd skidded on his knee across the cement and into the bark mulch, and I was on the spot when it all happened, so I pulled the syringe straight out. I'm not sure that he even noticed, and I didn't want to say anything in front of him. A lot of the kids know about the risks of needle-stick injuries these days. I'm sorry. I'm really sorry. We try to check the playground regularly, but—'

He looked ill with regret at having to give this news, and Aaron's mother had had to sit down.

'AIDS,' she said in a strangled voice.

Aimee saw Rebecca hiding her own concern and bringing all the vibrancy of her personality to the situation.

'Mrs Lloyd, the risk is very, very small,' she said quickly. 'It's a Monday morning. That needle has probably been in the mulch for at least a day, and yesterday was warm and sunny. Neither the AIDS virus nor hepatitis can survive in the absence of liquid, so as long as that syringe dried out thoroughly there's nothing to worry about.

'As well, Mr Perry's impression was that it hadn't gone in very far. Mrs Hilliard has just cleaned the whole area very thoroughly. We'll do a blood test, though, just to make sure. It'll take a week for a result to come through and then, just to make absolutely sure, we'll do another one in three months, but, as I said, the chances are *very* slight. I certainly wouldn't recommend alarming Aaron by telling him.'

'He's going to be alarmed enough by another needle,'

Mrs Lloyd joked shakily, her fears somewhat allayed by Rebecca's explanation.

And so Aimee took part in her third battle to administer a needle that morning. Yes, things definitely came in threes…

CHAPTER FOUR

AT THE beginning of her lunch-break, Aimee phoned Sarah to hear about her visit to her GP that morning. There wasn't much news as yet.

'He's sending me for another ultrasound, and he wants me to see an obstetrician. I've got a referral and I've made appointments.'

'Which obstetrician?'

'Well, I asked him about the husband of that doctor in your practice.'

'Marcus Gaines? He's married to Grace, who works here, yes.'

'Yes, and he said he was excellent. That is, Dr Maskell said Dr Gaines…Marcus Gaines…was—'

'I know what you meant,' Aimee said quickly. She could hear the false brightness in Sarah's tone. 'How are you feeling today?'

'Oh, OK…'

'Worse?' Aimee pushed.

'Yes, worse,' Sarah admitted. 'I'm glad Dr Maskell is sending me for a scan because it means he's taking it seriously…but I'm sorry he's taking it seriously, because it means he thinks there might be something wrong. I don't want there to be something wrong…but I know there is!'

When Aimee put down the phone a few minutes later, she felt like a wrung-out rag, and she must have looked like one, too, because Marshall came up to her and said quietly, 'Busy for lunch today?'

'No…'

'Want to come for soup and a sandwich on the beach?'

'Yes, please!'

He took her hand as soon as they were out the front door of the practice, and as they came down the steps Aimee saw Rebecca getting into her car, parked across the street. She looked across at them, and for a second her frown betrayed what she was thinking about those joined hands before it gave way to a bright smile and a wave.

'Enjoy your lunch,' she called.

'We will,' Marshall called back, caressing the back of Aimee's hand with his thumb, as if to reassure her.

Rebecca started her car, backed dangerously close to the car parked behind it, swung the wheel, then headed out into the street with a jerk and a protest of the engine. Aimee felt rather than heard Marshall's half-suppressed sigh, and she waited, expecting that he might say something about his daughter's ambivalent attitude.

He didn't, though, which somehow made Rebecca's attitude seem more significant, even though it wasn't a subject Aimee wanted to bring up herself. That was illogical of her, wasn't it?

They walked to a local sandwich shop and Marshall treated her like a convalescent who needed fattening up.

'Have the cream of pumpkin soup,' he urged her, 'and the sandwich special. Turkey breast, avocado...' He listed each ingredient, making them all sound utterly tempting, then finished. 'You look exhausted, Aimee.'

'I feel it,' she admitted, adding to the woman behind the counter, 'Yes, I'll have the special, too.'

'Would you like to go home for the afternoon? We can manage without you. We do on Wednesday and Friday afternoons, after all.'

'No, I'll be fine,' she said, 'and, since you've mentioned

it, Id like to start working a full day on Wednesdays and Fridays from now on, if I could.'

'Would you?'

'Well, you've said you'd like it if I did.'

'I know, but you mustn't feel pressured. We could always get someone else to fill in those—'

'No, I'd like to do it,' she interrupted, then feared that she'd sounded too insistent.

More and more strongly, she was feeling that she didn't want him to guess she was having financial problems. Not until she'd worked out for herself what it meant regarding their relationship. Why did she intuitively feel that it was going to make such a difference? It wasn't just the possibility of other people—Rebecca, for example—suspecting her of gold-digging. There was something else.

Marshall's hand closed around hers, warm and caressing, and one part of her instinctively felt that she should snatch it away, while another part wanted it to stay like that for hours. He was giving her all the support he could about Sarah, and his concern made such a difference.

Now he let his fingers slide gently away from her touch, and his arm slid around her shoulder, inviting her to lean into the strong yet trim bulk of his chest.

He felt and smelt familiar and good, and she gave in to her deep need for his support, letting her head rest against him for a moment so that she could feel the cool linen of his shirt against her cheek, then pulling away just a little. She could still feel his touch sending strength back into her limbs, but you couldn't have called it an embrace.

'Hard being a parent sometimes, isn't it?' Marsh said quietly after a few moments. They were still waiting for their soup and sandwiches. 'You think it won't be once they're grown up, but it still is. When they ache, we ache for them, all over again.'

'Only this time it isn't bumps and bruises and hurt feelings at school,' Aimee agreed.

'No, it's careers, or divorce, or something much bigger. I heard you talking to Sarah on the phone just now. Any news?'

'She's having another ultrasound, and her doctor has referred her to Marcus Gaines. That's all so far. I—I'm worried, Marsh. I wish there was something concrete to go on. Please, don't make me go home, because all I'll do there is dwell on it.'

'I won't make you go home,' he promised. 'In fact, I can think of some great ways to keep you from going home for days, if you're interested.'

The low, suggestively teasing comment had her laughing at last. 'What exactly did you have in mind?' she asked, as they took their soup cups and sandwich packets and left the shop to walk towards the grass and picnic benches that edged the sandy beach.

'Exactly?' He raised his eyebrow, and his drawl was full of meaning.

'Well, roughly, then.' She laughed again, and felt herself blushing. 'I suppose my imagination can fill in the gaps.'

'Mine can. I was going to start with suggesting dinner tonight at my place.'

'That sounds great.'

Almost like forbidden fruit. Tempting and fabulous, and not something she was certain she should accept. She saw the fire of pleasure flare in his eyes as they sat down at one of the benches.

'I'll make my specialty,' he said.

'Which is?'

He made a face. 'Actually, it's a tuna casserole, which my daughter tells me is hopelessly 1970s.'

'A tuna casserole sounds delicious,' she assured him

kindly, loving this small display of insecurity in his masculine ego. Did he really think she was going to judge him on the fashion status of his cooking?

He couldn't be too insecure on the subject, because he now proceeded to detail several other examples of his culinary repertoire which Rebecca found unacceptable, 'even though she wolfs every one of them down'. His humour was so delicious, particularly the saga of his experience with 'mock apple pie', that he had her in fits of laughter as she sipped her cup of soup—dangerous, that—and she almost forgot about all the issues that plagued her.

This had evidently been the intended effect, she realised when he sat back at last, his legs crossed lazily and both arms draped along the back of the wooden bench, to survey her with a twinkle in his blue eyes.

In the background, she heard the surf breaking rhythmically on the beach, each wave curling and swelling until it toppled over itself in a churning tumble of electric white foam. The sea breeze was gentle and fresh and salty, teasing at Marshall's grey-threaded hair, and the early August sunshine danced on the blue-green water, and in his eyes.

'That's better,' he said softly. 'Much better.'

'Oh, it is!' she agreed. 'Thank you. My face was aching from worry before, and my jaw was so tight…'

'Now you'll be able to chew on that sandwich.'

'I will!'

He leaned forward again and ran a finger back and forth very lightly across her knuckles as her hand rested on top of the sandwich bag.

'Don't ever think I'm not here to help,' he told her, his voice low and husky.

'Oh, Marsh, but I have *problems* at the moment,' she answered, feeling the relief at letting the words spill out. 'It's not fair to you, roping you into my life…'

He had stiffened a little. She felt it as if they'd been pressed length to length, only it was still just that one finger, stroking her hand with an erotic subtlety she'd never imagined before.

Alan, came the disloyal thought, with all his good qualities, had never been a subtle lover.

'It's not a question of being roped in, Aimee,' Marshall said very carefully. 'If you want me in your life, I want to be there. Is this about Friday night? Are you having regrets?'

The question was too sudden, too unexpected...and, since Peter's news, too accurate. When she had time to think about it, with so much of importance crowding her mind, yes, she wished that their night together hadn't happened. It had been utterly fabulous in itself, but as each hour went by the timing seemed more and more of a disaster.

She insisted to him, 'No, of course I'm not!' But there had been a hesitation, and he hadn't missed it.

There was no point in making the protest again. If she had any hope of easing his sudden flare of doubt, it would be through touch, so much more truthful than words.

She turned her hand so that his fingers rested on her palm, then took the weight of his hand in hers and lifted it to her shoulder. At the same time, she ran her other hand up his other arm, and pulled him close to her, in a gesture of open wanting that had him groaning with need before their lips met.

'Marshall...' It wasn't a particularly coherent use of his name, and her voice broke a little on the word.

'It's all right,' he said, in between his passionate onslaughts on her mouth. 'It's fine. I understand. Maybe I wouldn't even have wanted you to have no regrets. Because complicated feelings happen when something's important, don't they?'

'Yes. Oh, yes. Thank you for saying it.'

She let her lips map all the contours of his face, learning it off by heart with a desperation she didn't try to analyse just yet. The slight roughness of his jaw, the smooth hardness of his nose, the tickle of his eyelashes and the tenderness of the closed lids above. His hard temples, the lines of experience etched on his forehead and around his mouth, his hairline, and most of all his parted lips and the sweetness within.

Their kiss couldn't last for ever, but their closeness could last a little longer. She loved the way he managed to eat a thickly cut sandwich with one arm still around her shoulders, and he didn't let go of her until they were almost back at the surgery.

'Tonight?' he reminded her, pausing at the bottom of the steps. 'My place? Sevenish?'

'I'll be there,' she promised, forcing out all other thoughts, not letting herself think for one moment that this might be cowardice.

Aimee brought a chocolate cake to Marshall's that night.

She'd got to work on it almost obsessively the moment she'd arrived home from the practice, because she couldn't walk through the front door of her house now without the realisation flooding in. I have to sell my home, the place I've lived in for nearly thirty years, and there's no one I can talk to about it, no one who I can tell the whole story to.

So the chocolate cake was more like a piece of escapism than a piece of cookery but, of course, Marshall didn't know that.

'You didn't have to bring anything,' he told her, when

he saw the clingwrap-covered offering, still faintly warm from the oven and dusted with powdered sugar.

But, as she'd discovered over lunch, words had only a very distant relationship to truth. The boyish flash of hungry appreciation in his eyes told a very different story.

'Remembering your story of the mock apple pie made out of cracker biscuits, I have to tell you that this is my special recipe with mashed potato in it,' she said.

'My goodness!'

'Makes it wonderfully dense, which all good chocolate cakes should be.'

He took it from her and led the way through the house. Aimee had been here once before, some weeks ago, for drinks with everyone else in the practice, but she found herself taking in the details of the place and its furnishings with much more focus now.

The welcoming and slightly lived-in look was deceptive, she realised after he'd poured her a white wine and turned back to his salad preparations. There were several valuable pieces of antique furniture, and there was an original oil painting on the dining-room wall by a contemporary artist whose work, she'd recently read in the newspaper, now commanded very large prices indeed.

Oh, money! Curse the stuff! It was all she seemed to be able to think about at the moment, as if she had a cash register or a balance sheet in her head, and everything she saw or thought about had a price tag attached. How much would it cost, for example, to make Rebecca Irwin's ambivalent attitude go away?

Heavy, noisy things, cash registers. She was getting a headache, and some desperate gulps of her wine only made it worse. She carried on through the salad and the casserole, both delicious, letting Marshall do most of the talking, and foolishly took a piece of the cake as well, accompanied by tea.

But eventually she couldn't hide from the truth. This was a migraine, with all the embellishments—flickering vision, nausea and black, black pain.

She couldn't hide it from Marsh any longer either.

'You're not feeling well, are you?' he asked, eyeing her half-eaten piece of cake. They were still at the dining table, watched over by the expensive painting. She'd loved it at first, but now the bold arrangement of colour was like an alarm bell dinning in her brain.

'Migraine,' Aimee managed, but couldn't speak any more because of the nausea.

'I have some strong painkillers, with a light sedative in them. Will they take the edge off the pain enough for you to sleep it off if you lie down?'

'Probably.'

'You don't want to endure the journey home, do you?'

'No.'

'I didn't think so.'

It was wonderful not to have to explain to him what she needed. He helped her upstairs to the neat, cosy, spare room, which was furnished with an antique washstand, bowl and jug, amongst other things. She sat on the bed, not daring to move in case the pain and nausea overwhelmed her. He was back with the painkillers a minute later, and she downed two of them with a glass of water.

'Don't often get these…' she began to apologise.

'But when you do, they're corkers.' He nodded. 'I can tell. Don't say anything more—just lie down in the dark until the pain goes.'

At first, all she could do was lie utterly still, but gradually she felt the pills taking effect so that the pain was more bearable. The firm mattress was extremely comfortable, and the green and pink and yellow quilt on top of which she lay was puffy and soft. Snuggling into it more deeply, she heard Marshall say in the doorway, 'Here's another quilt to go on top. Don't want you to be cold.'

She murmured her thanks, and was going to say that she'd just snooze here for a minute or two and then she'd be able to go home, but the words were too heavy for her tongue to lift. Much too heavy. She'd say them later...

Aimee didn't wake again until morning. Early morning. There was just a glint of light appearing through the curtains, so it must be before six. Too early to get up, but much too late to go home. Poor Marsh! He might have wanted her to spend the night here, but she doubted whether this was what he'd envisaged!

Still, the headache was gone and she'd had more than nine hours of solid sleep, which had been badly needed. She lay in bed for another hour, with what had quickly become a predictable merry-go-round of concerns spinning in her head. The tension they generated battled with the sense of well-being created in her somehow just by knowing she was here under Marshall's roof.

As soon as she heard him moving about the house, she got up. Her clothing felt limp and creased, and her face and hair much the same, but that couldn't be helped. There wouldn't be time to go home and change with all the traffic surging across her route on its way to the city. But if she could just have a shower...

Marshall made an apologetic face when she suggested it. 'My shower's still out of action,' he said.

'Oh, your bathroom renovation—I'd forgotten!' she exclaimed.

'They can't start for another two weeks. But there's the tub in the bathroom downstairs.'

It would have to do. Then some coffee and a quick piece

of toast, and hopefully no one in the practice would notice that this was the same outfit of warm-toned skirt and white blouse she'd worn yesterday. At least she had a grey angora cardigan in the car which would camouflage the fact a little.

Marshall's downstairs bathroom was an old-fashioned one, opening off the back of the big kitchen. It must once have been a scullery, but had been upgraded some years ago. There was a big, deep tub, a toilet and basin, several house plants and a huge stained-glass window, through which the eastern winter sun came pouring, staining the cream-painted walls with red and blue and orange.

There was no modern nonsense about a single tap with a single control for hot and cold either. The separate hot and cold taps each had a generous flow, and the tub filled quickly. Aimee added a sachet of scented bath mousse, and had just stretched out in the tub with the taps turned off, feeling more relaxed than she'd expected to under the circumstances, when she heard a key rattling in a lock, the front door opening and the sound of Rebecca's voice.

'Dad?'

'Upstairs, gypsy,' he called down, his voice faint from where Aimee's was. 'What are you doing here so early?'

'Forgot I had a pre-natal at the health centre first thing,' she called back. 'And you wanted those files back this morning.'

'That's right. I've got Terry Lyons coming in. Did it help?'

'Looking at the files? Yes. I discovered I did know this stuff after all. I'm just putting them on the hall table, OK?'

'OK. See you at the surgery later on. Hope your pre-natal goes well.'

'It should,' she predicted blithely. 'Everything seems totally normal, and I've started feeling disgustingly good since I hit the thirteen-week mark last week.'

Aimee heard Marshall's chuckle, still echoing from his bedroom upstairs, and she expected to hear Rebecca's retreating feet and the sound of the front door again, but instead the footsteps came closer, their pace quickening.

Rebecca muttered. 'Ouch!' and something about her bladder, and then before Aimee had time to even realise what was about to happen, let alone react to it in any sensible manner, the bathroom door was wrenched open and she and Rebecca met each other's horrified faces.

Rebecca gasped, 'Oh, lordy-loo!'

She shut the door again and the footsteps resumed their urgent rhythm, this time leading up the stairs to the other bathroom.

Aimee felt like a fifty-year-old woman who'd just been caught naked in a bathtub on a Tuesday morning by her lover's daughter. Funny, that!

The relaxing influence of the scented bath water immediately vanished and she dragged herself quickly and clumsily from the tub, her skin squeaking across the porcelain as the water heaved, as if getting dried and dressed again as quickly as humanly possible might erase the event from time's annals altogether.

Her bra fastened crookedly, water still beading on her neck, briefs and pantihose dragged on as a single entity, skirt and blouse not meeting straight in the middle. She'd done it in two minutes.

She carried her shoes in her hand and tiptoed through the kitchen and along the hall like a cat-burglar, and only stopped when she reached the hall table and discovered that she hadn't left her handbag there last night as she'd thought. It must be on the end table in the lounge room instead. Or was it in the kitchen? Last night's migraine had pulled a curtain over her memory for details like that.

She paused to catch her breath and think, then heard Rebecca's voice beyond the top of the stairs.

'Not saying she'd take advantage of you financially, the way Tanya did, Dad, but—sorry, this is none of my business—'

'No, it *isn't*, gypsy,' Marshall cut his daughter off firmly. 'I thought we'd been through this twice already?'

Aimee couldn't bear to hear any more. Their voices were getting closer and they'd now reached the landing. She hurried back to the bathroom, closed the door silently, then began to run the taps in the tub again at full bore.

Turning them off several minutes later, she waited for quite some time before finally concluding from the sounds she heard in the kitchen that Rebecca had gone and Marshall was alone once more. Then she straightened her clothing, patted uselessly at her hair and went out to him with a big smile etched determinedly on her face, while her heart beat so heavily and painfully that she almost thought he'd be able to see it lurching against her ribs.

'Toast, cereal or eggs?' he offered her cheerfully. He had no idea that she'd overheard anything of what had just passed between himself and his daughter.

'Nothing, thanks,' she answered, the brightness of her voice too high-pitched. 'It's already almost eight o'clock. I'll go and open up the surgery and grab some coffee and biscuits while I set up.'

He looked at her sharply, alerted by something in her tone. 'Headache gone?'

'Quite gone,' she told him truthfully, and only realised at his next words that she'd missed an opportunity.

'Then you're bothered because Rebecca blundered in on you, aren't you?'

'It can't have been a pretty sight,' she joked feebly.

'Rebecca's a big girl,' he told her. His face had fallen into sober lines. 'She can handle it, Aimee.'

But she wouldn't have to.

Aimee knew now what the courageous part of her mind had been trying to tell her since yesterday morning. Perhaps even since Pete's news on Saturday. She couldn't just go blithely on with this...with Marsh...with what was happening.

It was too unfair. Unfair to everyone concerned. And there were so many people concerned in this! Sarah, Jason, Thomas and William. Rebecca and Harry and Marshall's son Simon. Everyone who worked at the practice. Two unborn children. Her brother. And Marsh and herself, perhaps, most of all.

I have to ask that we cool off. Break it off, I suppose is the phrase. Even though there's nothing to break. Nothing formal. Nothing openly stated between us at all, yet so much that *hasn't* been spoken. Oh, it would be so much easier if he hadn't stayed last Friday night!

Then I have to get the rest of my life under control. Sell the house and work out what I can afford to rent. Make sure I can make ends meet, and that the children make good use of their money from the house. I can't tell Marsh why. I can't tell him that I'm broke. That'd be like fishing for an assurance that it didn't matter, and it does.

Rebecca has made that only too clear, but I knew it anyway. For her it might be the fortune-hunting issue. For me it's something different, but it's just as strong. Stronger!

I wanted equality between Marsh and myself. Not some political interpretation of that word, but simply the knowledge that we were both coming to the relationship freely, with an equal amount to give.

Oh, yes, in this case, money matters, and I don't have any, and I have to deal with it on my own, learn to live with what I do have and attain a true sense of independence for the very first time in my life!

If I don't, if I just use the fact that Marsh has money as an easy way out of my own problems, then our relationship will inevitably be built on exactly the same foundation as Alan's and my marriage was, and I just don't want that a second time! I don't. For all sorts of reasons.

'I expect she can.' Aimee answered Marshall's assurance about Rebecca more calmly and easily than she felt. 'But, to be honest, I think she's right to be shocked. We—we've jumped into this too soon, Marshall.'

She saw the alarm in his eyes and ploughed on. Better to get it over with!

'I—I'm sorry,' she stammered, appalled by how hard it was, by how attractive was the picture in her mind of what might have been. 'This is my fault. I should have thought about it more carefully before I—well, before I let my—physical needs...dictate the pace.'

Oh, lord, this was almost impossible! She stared down at her hands, twisting convulsively together, the way her body and his had twisted together last Friday night. The memories flooded in, every one of them emotional and wonderful. The words he'd used, the way he'd made sure every touch was welcome and right. His abandonment, there in the darkness, as they'd joined together. His tenderness afterwards, and the trusting way he'd slept in her arms.

Say it right, she coached herself. Be as truthful as you can without giving him a reason to challenge it. Don't let him think if he argues...or takes me into his arms...I might change my mind. Because I might! And that can't happen. I'd never be able to hold my head up again as I faced myself in the mirror each day.

'What are you saying, Aimee?' Marsh questioned quietly, and she heard the friction in his throat. He'd abandoned his breakfast preparations, but hadn't yet put down a butter knife. It hung uselessly in his fingers. 'This seems a little sudden, and I'd...like to make sure I've understood.'

'It isn't sudden,' she blurted. 'What we started was sudden, and I think it was a mistake. I don't want an involvement with you. I'm not looking for something like this in my life... I can't.' She had to harden her voice to keep the tears back, and it came out quite harshly. 'I shouldn't have let it get this far.'

He was too much of a gentleman to show his hurt. Too much of a gentleman, and too sensitive, in the best way a man could be, to argue with her.

'Thank you for telling me what you feel, then,' he said. 'For telling me straight away. Thank you for your honesty. I appreciate...' he cleared his throat '...that you didn't...simply stop returning my phone calls, or something.' He tried to laugh, but didn't quite succeed.

'No, well, I—'

'No hard feelings. Sometimes these things don't work out. Sometimes people don't know what they want until they try it.'

'Thank you for—'

'No, I—'

Neither of them had the slightest idea what they were trying to say any more. Every inch of Aimee's skin was burning, and Marshall had turned to the toaster, from which a transparent plume of blue smoke was now rising.

'Damn!' he said, more to himself than Aimee. 'It doesn't pop up half the time these days. Place is falling down around my ears!'

'I'll go and open up the surgery. Would you like me to take those files Rebecca left on the hall table?'

'Thanks.'

'I'll see you shortly, then,' she said.

'Mmm.'

'Thank you for—'

'Aimee!' There was agony in his voice now, and his shoulders were set stiffly. He still had his back to her so she couldn't see his expression. The kitchen smelt of burnt toast. She could imagine his face, though, and the same expression would have been on her face, too, if she hadn't been controlling it so rigidly. 'For heaven's sake, will you stop now? Stop thanking me? It's fine, all right?'

'I'm sorry, I—'

'And apologising. Please...' He took a jagged breath and started again. 'Please, just go!'

She did, without another word.

CHAPTER FIVE

'PHONE for you, Aimee. Can you take it now?' said Deirdre, one of the practice's four part-time receptionists, just before lunch. 'It's your daughter.'

'I'll pick it up in the treatment room,' Aimee said, crossing the corridor. She'd been shelving some newly arrived supplies, and had no more patients to see before lunch.

In the treatment room, she closed the door then snatched up the phone. 'Sarah?'

But Deirdre hadn't put the call through yet. A few seconds later, there was a click and an impatient, 'Hello?' at the other end of the line.

'Yes, it's me, love,' Aimee said.

'Oh, Mum, good!'

'You've had the ultrasound, and seen Dr Gaines?'

'Yes, he came and looked at the scan while I was having it. We didn't have to go to his office. We've just got home.'

She sounded shaky but not tearful, calmer than she'd been yesterday, and her explanation was almost too lucid, too clinical.

'The technician measured the amniotic fluid,' she went on. 'It's an estimate, really, not a measurement. They plot the distance from the baby to the wall of the uterus in four different spots, and then average it out to get a result in millimetres. You probably know this.'

'Some of it. Tell me anyway.'

'That gives them this thing they call... Oh, hell, what is it?' Her superficial control began to break down. Aimee heard Jason's voice in the background. 'That's right,' Sarah went on. 'The amniotic fluid index. Sounds like something that should be on the stock exchange, doesn't it? Anyway, the normal range is ten to twenty-five millimetres.'

'And what are you?'

'Thirty-eight.'

'Too much.'

'Dr Gaines says they'll monitor it. It's not necessarily significant. I'm going to have a scan every two weeks. If it gets worse they may have to drain it. But they don't want to because that might trigger labour, and it's too soon. So they'll hold off as long as they can. By the way, we decided we might as well find out the sex after all. It's a girl!'

'Oh, love, how wonderful! That's what you were hoping for, isn't it?'

'It was. It still is. I suppose. I would have loved a boy, too. Right now all I care about is that things are OK. Dr Gaines says I'm supposed to rest a lot.'

'And that's all?'

There was a pause. 'No. It's not all. He's concerned because he couldn't see the stomach on the ultrasound. The baby's stomach.'

'Yes...'

'It should have partly filled, you see, because babies swallow amniotic fluid in the womb.'

'That's right.'

'And then the stomach should show up nicely on the scan. But this time it didn't. He was very calm, Mum.'

Sarah wasn't. Not underneath. Aimee wasn't fooled about that for a second.

'And so I honestly don't know,' Sarah went on. 'Perhaps Dr Gaines knows exactly what's wrong and he's not prepared to tell us.'

'Doctors aren't usually like that these days,' Aimee soothed. 'If he knew something definite, he'd tell you.'

'No, well, it was all maybes. He says there might be a problem with the oesophagus. That the baby can't swallow. *She* can't swallow.' Sarah laughed shakily, and added as an aside, 'Feels funny, suddenly, knowing the sex.'

'I never did, with the three of you.'

Sarah returned to her report. 'Because of a blockage, or maybe a growth, which they would deal with surgically after the birth,' she said. 'As soon as the baby was strong enough. It's… I can't imagine it. Surgery. On my baby. So small. But Dr Gaines just keeps talking in possibilities.'

Her voice had risen now. Aimee heard Jason in the background again, and added her own reassurance.

'That's all he can do, love,' she said. 'Just do as he says, and take it easy.'

'I'm going to. I've—I've made a decision actually. Well, Jason agrees. I'm going to leave work.'

'You mean resign?'

'Yes. I hadn't planned to. I mean, I've been researching child-care centres, I was going to go back to work full time six weeks after the birth, like a career superwoman. You know, proving myself for the sake of all womankind. But… Oh, you haven't got time to hear this now.'

Aimee assured Sarah that she did. She'd barely had breakfast, and now she was late for lunch, but her appetite had fled hours ago during her painful conversation with Marshall in his kitchen, so it hardly seemed to matter. Sarah didn't manage to articulate her feelings very clearly, but Aimee understood.

'It might have been different if the pregnancy had been easy,' Sarah said. 'But it isn't. It hasn't been, all along…and it's made me realise…anything can happen when you have a child, and I don't want to be in a situation where I can't take extra time for my baby if I need to. Only the thing is, Mum, financially…' That word again! Aimee already hated the very sound of it. 'We took out our mortgage on the assumption we'd have two incomes. I mean, we'll manage… I can do part-time work probably, if I have to, but—'

'You won't have to,' Aimee said quickly. 'Of all things, that's not something I want you to worry about!'

And she told Sarah about the true ownership of the Woollahra house, what Alan had wanted—which she herself was determined to respect, no matter what it cost her, although she didn't say any of this to Sarah—and that if the children all agreed, she was ready—indeed, determined—to sell.

The house was miles too big for her, she finished firmly, and she was ready for a change.

Outside the treatment room, on his way between his office and the practice's little kitchen, and then back again with his sandwich and his tea, Marshall heard the changing emotions expressed in Aimee's voice—anxiety, love, enthusiasm, determination—and wondered what they all meant.

He didn't allow himself to listen to the words. In the most encouraging of circumstances, he wasn't an enthusiast for eavesdropping, and it would be unconscionable to do it now.

But, oh, he would have liked to!

Her announcement this morning had come at him like a charging bull in a serene, flower-filled meadow, totally unexpected and every bit as unwelcome. He'd had no inkling that she wasn't as serious about what they'd begun to build together as he was. Now he had this horrible and, no doubt, all too stiff-necked male need to look for clues to the matter, as if this were one of the detective novels he read occasionally, and somewhere there was a key to a mystery.

He chided himself. Why couldn't he accept the situation at face value? Wouldn't he expect a woman to, if their positions were reversed? But all the rationalising and inner arguing in the world didn't do a thing for the aching and pulling of his heart.

He'd begun to love Aimee Hilliard, and he didn't know how he was going to stop.

'Oh, look, it's a lovely place,' the well-groomed real-estate agent, Monica Farwell, said. 'There are the problems with the roof and the driveway and the back fence, which will bring down your price somewhat, and the bathroom and kitchen need modernising. But most people buying into this area want to renovate in any case. I could see a deck off the dining room, I could see an extension to take advantage of the northern sun. It's just possible you might squeak in a square inch of harbour view, which, of course, is gold in Sydney.'

'I don't think so,' Aimee had to say. 'I don't think the house is quite high enough.'

'No? Oh, well…'

The agent clicked about in her high heels, measuring the rooms with a special electronic laser device and scribbling the figures down. Aimee had already explained that she'd like a quick sale, if possible, and had been persuaded that an auction was the way to go, 'with pre-auction offers considered', Mrs Farwell had suggested.

'It'll be snapped up,' she'd also said, 'and at a price you wouldn't have dreamed of ten years ago.'

She'd offered to show Aimee other units to buy, and hadn't quite hidden her surprise at Aimee's firm statement that she would be renting.

'Well, it does make sense to take it slowly, rather than rushing into a new purchase,' she had said, 'but ultimately you'd be mad not to.'

Aimee had let that go. There were many things she was learning to let go. Like Marshall's quiet comment last Friday, 'You're selling your house, I hear. Not thinking of moving away?'

'No. Just down-sizing to something smaller.' That was all she'd allowed herself to say.

It was Monday evening now, just a week since she'd spent the night at Marshall's place, sleeping off her migraine, and the house would be open for exhibition this Saturday. She desperately wanted to move quickly with it all, get the upheaval over and done with, relieve Sarah's money worries at least, and burn her own boats so that she wasn't ever weakly tempted to believe she'd been wrong to tell Marshall what she had.

Thomas and William had both agreed to the sale, and were pleased about the financial nest-egg for their future. Studying for his doctorate in zoology, and still away in Queensland, Thomas was relieved, over the phone, at the thought of being able to get through his three remaining years of study without taking out more student loans. William was talking about investments in a hazy yet determined manner.

Because Aimee had been so careful to present the plan in an upbeat, enthusiastic way, and because the three children all assumed her own financial future to be very comfortably taken care of, none of them had asked any awkward questions or suggested giving any of the sale's proceeds back to Aimee, and she wouldn't have accepted the money if they had.

She hadn't enjoyed the past week at work. It was strange how she hadn't realised the full importance to her of

Marshall's presence at the practice, and how pleasantly it had coloured each day.

Did I feel like this about him from the beginning, then? she'd wondered helplessly. Before I even realised it? Perhaps I did. Even that first day at my job interview, I remember... She'd come away from it with a slightly flustered and very alive feeling which she'd put down at the time purely to the prospect of landing a good and permanent job.

By the end of the previous week, she'd been exhausted by the effort of relating to Marshall in the courteous, professional way they both wanted, and she wasn't quite sure how she would manage to keep it up. He'd behaved impeccably, but would that all end with her having to leave the practice? The possibility loomed like a grey cloud, twinned with the cloud of worry over Sarah's baby.

'I have everything I need for the leaflet now,' Mrs Farwell said. 'And we're agreed on the price you're hoping for. We did the paperwork the other day. All set, then!'

'Lovely,' Aimee said automatically.

Ten days later, on a Thursday in mid-August, the week after Marshall's run in Sydney's annual City to Surf race—he'd placed in the top thousand runners, he'd announced in a satisfied tone last Monday morning—she'd accepted a pre-auction offer for the house. She'd also agreed on a settlement date and begun to pack, though she hadn't yet begun looking for a place to rent.

She hadn't had time, and her cash flow was in an alarming state. One credit card was teetering on the edge of its limit, another was mounting in charges daily as the tradesmen's bills came in for the cosmetic work she'd had done on the house. She'd already scaled down her estimate of the monthly amount she could afford to pay in rent.

On the other hand, the boys were pleased at how

smoothly everything was proceeding, and still hadn't asked any awkward questions. Thomas was miles away in body, and William appeared to be miles away in spirit at the moment. In his case, Aimee suspected a serious case of blissful first love. Preoccupied with his own changed financial circumstances, Pete hadn't expressed any concerns. Sarah was the one who might have questioned the speed of it all, but she was in no fit state to think beyond the constant discomfort of her own body and the specialist's concerns about the health of the baby that grew inside her.

The news following another ultrasound that morning wasn't good. Marcus Gaines still couldn't find any evidence that the baby was swallowing normally and filling its stomach, and Sarah's amniotic fluid index was now up to fifty millimetres.

Jason phoned the news to Aimee at lunchtime, and reported, 'They're going to try and drain off some of the fluid, but we're pretty scared. Apparently, it could trigger labour, and she's only at thirty weeks. The thing is…' he laughed jaggedly '…if they don't drain it and the pressure builds any further, it could trigger labour anyway.'

'Are they going to keep her in overnight?'

'Yes, or a couple of days,' he said, then added distractedly, 'I have to go. They're ready to start and she wants me there.'

'Of course.' Aimee's voice fogged. 'I'm thinking of you both, Jase. You have all my love. And so does the baby.'

After she'd put down the phone she had to stand with her back to the waiting room for several minutes, trying not to cry and wishing she'd had the sense to take the phone call somewhere private, rather than snatching up the receiver here at the desk as soon as Bev had told her Jason was on the line.

At least the place was quiet—no patients, and most of

the staff away buying their lunch or doing errands. She'd just finished her own pre-lunch tidying before Jason had phoned. She'd been about to make a trip to the bank, but that could wait. She didn't want to deal with it now. As for lunch, she had a sandwich in her bag, but it didn't appeal right now.

She heard footsteps behind her, coming from along the corridor, and could tell without looking that it was Marshall.

'Is it Sarah, Aimee?' he said.

She nodded, forcing back the tears. I can't cry in front of him because then he'll take me in his arms and…

He didn't, though. He'd been so scrupulous and careful about keeping his distance these past two weeks, a model of courtesy and honour. How was it possible, then, that she could still feel his tenderness and care as strongly as if she had her face pressed into his chest and his fingers caressing her hair.

'Her fluid level has jumped,' she reported to him. In many ways, words were much easier than silence. 'The A.F.I. is fifty millimetres. She has to have it drained, and I'm so afraid—'

'That it could be born early,' he finished for her. 'How far along is she?'

'Thirty weeks.'

'The odds these days are very, very good,' he said, striding much closer to her in his concern. He was beside her now, close enough to touch, although neither of them did. She didn't look at him either, just kept staring down at the silent telephone, fiddling with its cord. 'Most babies born at thirty weeks not only survive but have no enduring problems at all.'

'Even if they're born with oesophageal atresia?' she

questioned harshly, making the quarter turn that would bring them face to face.

His silence and clamped jaw told her how she had shocked him, but he recovered quickly. 'Are they sure?'

'Not absolutely.' She looked up at him. 'But it's becoming a strong possibility. They think they won't know for certain until the baby's born, Jason said, and, of course, it's a condition that can vary considerably in severity.'

'Depending on the gap between the two unfinished sections,' he said, nodding, illustrating the problem with his hands almost automatically, the way he would have done if he'd been explaining something to a patient. 'The smaller the gap, the better. And there can sometimes be a fistula between the windpipe and the oesophagus.'

'Yes, and they've said there could also be a blockage on the way out of the stomach to the duodenum as well.'

'Yes, it's all part of the same condition. A statistical abnormality, not a genetic one, it's believed,' Marshall said.

He had his hand resting on the high front desk now, making Aimee aware of how much she liked the lean shape of his fingers and the knotty arrangement of veins and sinew between knuckles and wrist. She remembered all too clearly how those hands had touched her—by turns gentle, questing, ardent, feverish, sleepy.

There was another silence. Aimee felt just a tiny bit better about Sarah and the baby. It helped just to put the situation into words, helped to know that Marsh cared, even though she couldn't let herself respond to it as she so badly wanted to.

'Let me know if there's anything I can do,' he added at last.

To Marshall's own ears, his voice sounded impossibly stiff, but Aimee simply nodded and he saw that she was still struggling against tears.

Bleakly, he thought, She hardly knows I'm here. If I'm any use to her at all, it's purely as a doctor, because I can give the sort of reassurance about favourable statistics and the brilliance of today's surgeons that I've been giving to patients or their relatives for years.

I always mean it, and I mean it so very much when I say it to her, but she's hardly noticed, and I can't hate her for that. She has all this worry, and it's not as if she's been unfair. She decided a relationship between us wasn't going to work, and she told me so straight away. What more could I have asked for?

That she love me. And that I understood why it wasn't working for her!

He pushed away this pained cry from the heart, schooling himself against the hurt and...even worse...the sheer bewilderment.

Aimee wasn't like Tanya, who'd used him as far as she'd dared and had then put on a show of angry affront in order to end the charade. Aimee was a mature, sincere, caring woman, and someone who should have known her own mind. Yet she'd acted like a teenager, blowing hot, then cold.

Yes, he was bewildered, and he didn't dare show it, not to Aimee herself and particularly not to Rebecca because—this was ironic—he knew how angry Rebecca would be on his behalf, and he wanted to *protect* Aimee from that.

Yet strangely, he thought, managing to laugh to himself, there were still some people who insisted that it was the female of the species that was illogical when it came to their emotions!

Shaking his head helplessly, he groaned aloud.

'Dad?' Rebecca pounced on him, emerging from her office like a dragon from its lair. He hadn't realised that she was in there, and had simply been wandering aimlessly back down the corridor towards his office, lost in the turmoil of his thoughts. 'Are you all right?'

'I'm fine,' he said heartily.

'What were you muttering, then?'

'Nothing.'

She studied him with narrowed, glittering eyes, saying nothing. 'No, really,' she said at last. 'It's not nothing. What is it?'

'I'm seeing Joan Allyson this afternoon,' he improvised. 'She's going on her honeymoon to Africa and I'm just running through the list of shots and pills I have to give her. It's a little bit frightening. I hope she knows what she's in for. If I were off on a honeymoon, I have to say I'd have settled on a nice, luxurious, self-contained cottage on the Barrier Reef somewhere, or an air-conditioned hotel in Hawaii.'

'Are you planning a honeymoon, then?' Rebecca demanded.

'No. I'm not,' he replied bleakly, and realised too late how much he'd given away.

'No, somehow I got the impression that you weren't,' his daughter muttered with a grim expression. 'I'd better get some lunch or I'll faint. This baby's growing. I wish Harry wasn't off today!'

'Rebecca, don't—'

But she didn't stay to hear about what she wasn't to do. Ducking back into her office, she grabbed her bag from the hook behind the door and marched off down the corridor with a set to her shoulders that told him more clearly than any words could have done that she was intending to behave badly.

It was something he'd very firmly resolved not to do himself. In fact, it was the only thing keeping him going at the moment, an Englishman's sense of honour, a stiff upper lip, and it was damned hard, so he shut himself in his office and sat for a few moments at his desk with his head buried in his hands, daydreaming that he was a man of hot-blooded Mediterranean lineage in times gone by and could throw Aimee over the back of a black stallion, carry her off into the night and make her admit that she loved him in a voice that was breathless and trembling with the force of her desire…

Out in the waiting room, Rebecca was saying with bright, ruthless politeness to Aimee, 'Have you set up the trolley for the removal of Mrs Fox's basal cell carcinoma yet, Aimee? I'm going to need it straight after lunch.'

It sounded like a veiled accusation, and Aimee flinched. 'I'm planning to take a break now, and do it as soon as I've had my sandwich.'

'All right. That's fine. I'll expect to find it ready when I get back.'

The pregnant doctor went out the front door without another word, only a staccato rattling of the wooden Venetian blinds as terse punctuation to her words. There had been nothing amiss about the content of her conversation, but the tone left much to be desired.

Alone in the waiting room, Aimee sagged against the high front desk, certain about what it meant.

Rebecca knew!

She'd been wondering if Marshall had said anything to his daughter. There had been some curious and increasingly suspicious glances from Rebecca over the past two weeks, as well as some apparently casual questions about how Aimee had spent her weekend, which Aimee had fielded as best she could.

To be fair, Aimee had seen how hard Rebecca was struggling to remain pleasant, especially in front of the rest of the practice staff, who might have suspected but didn't know for certain, but just now the façade had dropped and her hostility had shown through.

Marshall and Rebecca must have talked about it, Aimee realised. He's either told her straight out that we're not seeing each other any more or she's guessed and, of course, she blames me. She's right to, but, oh, it's not what she thinks!

And, she remembered, Rebecca hadn't exactly been jumping for joy about the issue even when everything had seemed rosy. It made Aimee's decision seem, in hindsight, like the only possible one she could have made. But to realise that Marshall's daughter disliked her so strongly was a bitter form of vindication.

'How are you today, Joan?' Marshall asked his patient.

She looked a little tired and unhappy, in contrast to her last visit when she'd seemed so healthy and radiant. Surely something can't have gone wrong in so short a time? he wondered.

Then his stomach lurched as he thought of himself and Aimee, and how suddenly that had turned sour. He still didn't know why, and didn't know if there was any point in trying to work it out.

Joan sat down opposite his desk. 'I'm a bit concerned,' she admitted, then added, 'I'll be honest, I'm terrified! The mammogram I had... I got the result last Friday and something showed up. I had to go to the assessment clinic again on Tuesday and have a core biopsy.'

'And you're still waiting for the results?' Marshall guessed. 'I'm sorry, Joan. Waiting for something like that is terrible, isn't it? Time goes so slowly.'

'They say I should hear by tomorrow afternoon,' she said.

'You must be sore still?'

'Yes, quite sore. And I don't suppose the vaccination shots will help!'

'Do you know what I think?' he said slowly, 'Let's not do them today. I know you're pressed for time, with the wedding coming up, but let's make another appointment for Monday—wait for the results of the biopsy first.'

Joan looked frightened. 'I suppose... Oh, hell, if it *is* something, you're saying I won't even need the shots because I won't be going to Africa after all.'

'It's possible,' he admitted. 'Although I'd been thinking more that you wanted to heal from the biopsy before you put your body through a possible reaction to the shots. Let's take things one at a time.'

'That makes sense.' She nodded. 'I'm getting wedding jitters. Shouldn't be, at fifty-eight, but I am. Keep feeling as if I need to be doing ten things at once or I'll run out of time. I tell you, anyone who thinks love is any more comfortable the second time around hasn't actually been through it!'

Marshall summoned a chuckle from some resourceful core of his spirits and sent Joan on her way.

'Phone when you get the biopsy result,' he said to her as she left. 'They'll send a copy here eventually, but I'd like to know as soon as you do.'

Aimee was in the treatment room, tidying up after the skin cancer removal that Rebecca had just done. Rebecca handled minor surgery of this type with practised ease and efficiency these days.

Aimee looked up at Marshall as soon as he appeared in the doorway.

'I have everything ready for Joan now,' she said.

'She won't be needing it today after all,' Marshall told her, schooling his voice carefully.

He reacted every time he saw her, his memory of her

body in his arms so vivid, triggered by the cool, floral scent she used. It came clearly to his nostrils as she moved, despite the competing medicinal scents of the treatment room. His fingers tingled when he remembered how he'd run them through the silver silk of her hair. His mouth remembered the warmth of her neck, her face, her breasts. And he was utterly determined to let none of this show.

'She's waiting for the result of a left breast core biopsy she had on Tuesday,' he explained, seeking refuge in the familiar clinical terminology.

'Oh, no!'

'Yes, there didn't seem much point in doing her shots yet, but let's hope we can reschedule them for next week and she'll get some good news.'

Aimee nodded, and he could tell that her mind had returned to her daughter and the news she was waiting for herself.

'Nothing to report on Sarah yet?' he couldn't resist asking.

'Nothing yet,' she echoed. 'Sorry, Marsh, I'm on tenterhooks. Wasting company time,' she joked feebly. 'Jason said he'd call as soon as he could. If the drain does trigger her labour, it could happen any time in the next forty-eight hours, they've told him, so I'm not going to be remotely livable with for another two days!'

As if their talking about it had made it happen, the phone rang in the treatment room at that moment. Aimee picked it up, listened for a moment, then said, 'Yes Bev, put him through.'

Marshall felt his feet put down roots here in the doorway. He had a patient waiting, but this would only take a minute. He didn't even question whether he had the right to listen in like this.

'Jason?' Aimee demanded shakily. 'How did it go?'

She was intently focused on the call, the fine skin around her mouth tight and her pupils dilated, darkening those sparkling crystal blue eyes. 'Uh-huh… That's a lot… Was it? But she's—?' A long pause to listen. 'OK, I'm glad they're keeping her in. I'll be there straight after work. Look after her, Jase… Yes, I know you will. I love you both. And that baby! Bye.'

When she'd put down the phone, she let her hand rest on it for a moment, and Marshall noticed for the first time that she still wore her wedding and engagement rings, but on her right hand now. He wondered—looking for clues again—if it was significant. How could he have missed a detail like that for so long? Especially when he loved her fine, long fingers so much, with their tapering nails coated in clear polish.

'Sorry.'

She looked up at him, treating his presence as a natural thing, which both warmed and disturbed him. He had no real right to expect to be the first to hear the news. She shouldn't want him to be here! If she didn't want him in her life, why wasn't she pushing him away as she had two and a half weeks ago? That would have made things a hell of a lot easier!

'Don't apologise,' he said awkwardly, feeling himself at sea amidst all these waves of conflicting emotions. 'Just tell me what's going on.'

'They drained off almost three litres of fluid,' Aimee reported. 'She had some contractions, but they've given her a drug to try and relax the uterus and ease the pain. Touch and go. She's had the shakes quite badly, Jason said.'

'They probably used Ventolin,' Marshall offered. 'That's a side effect of it in her situation.'

Aimee nodded. 'OK. I didn't know that.'

'But no definite signs of labour?'

'Not yet. They're going to keep her in overnight. Jason said he could see her belly getting smaller and softer as the fluid drained.'

'She'll feel a lot more comfortable.'

'I hope so.'

'Don't worry about it, Aimee.'

Oh, just listen to that priceless pearl of wisdom! he chided himself. Can't you do better than that?

She gave an absent smile and he got himself away before he said something even more puerile, feeling like a sixteen-year-old boy trapped in a mature man's body.

He hated his gender at the moment, and his upbringing. Who could he talk to? No one! Women had friends to whom they bared their hearts. Aimee had a daughter. He could imagine her in his position, talking it all over with Sarah, both of them possessed of an innate talent for expressing the complexity of it, arriving at some sense of understanding and peace.

Had she already talked to Sarah about her own perspective? Could he attempt the same thing?

He thought of Rebecca and at once knew it was impossible. She was too partisan, too hostile. She would condemn Aimee utterly, and that wasn't what he needed to hear. The last thing he wanted was to end up hating her. Rebecca's husband Harry, then?

No.

It was a notional possibility. The two of them were playing golf together this Saturday. Marshall had introduced his son-in-law to the game. Since Rebecca categorically refused to set foot on a golf course these days, he and Harry could do the heart-to-heart thing as they toiled from tee to green, but…oh, it would be ghastly! Two or three terse, masculine remarks ending in a mutual agreement that women were a mystery known only to themselves. He'd feel naked and foolish, and to what end?

Striding with false efficiency along to the waiting room to collect his next patient, Marshall encountered the practice's fourth partner, Grace Gaines, who said in a teasing tone, 'Cheer up, Marsh, it may never happen,' before doing a double take and adding far more seriously. 'Actually, is everything all right?'

'All right? I wouldn't be dead for quids!' he answered, using a colloquial Australian expression that he'd never used before in his life.

Using it convincingly, too, it seemed. Grace chuckled and went on her way, seeking out Aimee in the treatment room.

'Could I get you to take a patient history for me, Aimee?' he heard her ask in a chirpy tone.

Grace had been a different woman for the past few days, with a new spring to her step and a soft glow in her face, warming to a secret, happy smile whenever she thought no one was looking. Marshall guessed that she and her husband Marcus must have sorted out their long-standing and very real problems at last.

Grace had lost a baby *in utero* just five weeks from her due date last year, and it had nearly broken her marriage apart. There had been a six-month separation, followed by a fraught reconciliation.

Marshall was very happy for both Grace and Marcus that they'd worked things out—and he was envious, too. When you had a marriage, you could do that. Work on it. There was a shared and acknowledged base of love and commitment and past history together. He didn't have that with Aimee. All he had was the tantalising, mocking promise of their wonderful beginning…their weekend in the mountains…their night together. And it counted for nothing now that Aimee had so firmly and suddenly closed the door on it.

Alone with his patient, he began with a briskness that he didn't feel, 'Now, Mr Martin, how can I help you today?'

In the treatment room, Aimee gave Grace a far briefer summary on Sarah's condition than she'd given Marshall.

'I've been thinking of her, and of you,' the red-headed doctor said, with the gleam of tears in her eyes. 'Marcus will do the very best he can, of course. I don't think Sarah will be sorry she chose him. He always was a caring doctor, but he's said that losing our baby made him understand just how hard it can be for people when things go wrong.'

'I've told Sarah about that. I—I hope you don't mind,' Aimee said, suddenly afraid that she might have been unintentionally breaking a confidence when she'd only been trying to give Sarah some extra reassurance about Dr Gaines's sensitivity.

'Not at all,' Grace answered. 'We're both…a lot more at ease talking about James's death these days.' His name flowed comfortably from her lips, her tone filled with warmth. 'It's good, in a way, to feel that his little life meant something to other people, even if it's only that Marcus and I both understand our patients' feelings far better now.'

'Tell me about the patient you want me to see,' Aimee said quickly.

'She's Egyptian,' Grace answered. She seemed to understand Aimee's need to get back to business. 'Her English is so-so. She's young and keen to work on it, and she's determined not to use an interpreter, but her history is complicated, I gather from her husband, and I really want to take the time to get it right. If you can go through it very slowly and carefully and write it all down. Anything that's contradictory or unclear, flag it for me so I can double-check. I'd hate to miss something, as I'm going to be seeing her regularly for a while, with referrals to specialists as well.'

And so the afternoon passed. Aimee spent nearly an hour on Omnia Bostros's history, having to excuse herself twice during that time to help Rebecca with other patients. In the end, Grace was very pleased with the detail and clarity she'd obtained, covering a series of childhood illnesses, two operations following an accident and some treatment for infertility in Egypt which Grace apparently felt hadn't necessarily been indicated at that stage.

Late in the day, Aimee recognised Marshall's patient Hilde Deutschkron in the waiting room, accompanied by her daughter. Mrs Deutschkron didn't look well, and her daughter didn't look happy.

Neither did Marshall after he'd seen them, and Aimee couldn't help asking, 'Has she made a decision about the chemotherapy yet?'

'Yes,' he said, then sighed. 'She's not going to have it.'

'You were hoping she would?'

He headed in the direction of the kitchen to make himself a cup of coffee and she went with him as he seemed to expect it. In fact, she saw, he was making two cups. She didn't protest!

'I don't know,' he answered her. 'I'm not sure why I'm feeling the way I am. I'd have thought this was a decision I'd support. Acceptance, instead of a difficult fight that won't give her much more time. But I suppose I felt that *she* wasn't entirely happy with her decision.'

'What makes you think that?' Aimee asked.

He thought for a moment, then answered, 'She said it so defiantly, as if she was asking...almost begging...for a good reason to feel differently, only I wasn't able to give her one. She's always taken such pride in her will for survival, her capacity to fight. This doesn't feel like a decision made from the heart, but one from the head, and I'm always sceptical of the human brain when it dictates something in opposition to a heart that's been a very successful, intuitive organ in the past.'

Aimee was silent at this, winded by the way his words reflected her own feelings about him. She'd made a decision with her brain that *was* right, but it didn't stop the protesting of her heart all the same.

'You expressed that very well,' she told him at last.

'Did I?'

Marshall smiled briefly as he poured boiling water over the dark brown granules of instant coffee. They hissed a little, and the water steamed invitingly, then he splashed milk in on top. Some of it spilled, but he didn't react, just picked up his cup and left the kitchen, so that their conversation hung in the air, dissatisfying and unfinished.

Just like their relationship.

Aimee wiped up the spill for him, took one mouthful of the coffee then tipped the rest down the sink, her stomach rebelling.

CHAPTER SIX

'MRS DEUTSCHKRON, I was a little worried to see your name on my appointment list again so soon,' Marshall said to his elderly patient on Friday morning.

It was less than twenty-four hours since her last visit, and Deirdre had had to squeeze her in between two long-standing appointments. She didn't have her daughter with her, and she'd come by taxi.

He was already feeling less than brilliant this morning. He'd asked Aimee about her visit to Sarah last night, and had received only a brief, sanitised reply, as if she regretted the way she'd let him into her personal life yesterday.

Sarah was much more comfortable, Aimee had said. Her uterine contractions had settled. There was no cervical dilatation. Marcus was cautiously optimistic, and Jason and Sarah were both in good spirits.

'So I might actually be able to earn my keep in this practice today, you'll be pleased to hear!' she'd finished, as if he'd only asked because he was keeping tabs on her performance.

Her wilful misreading of his motives saddened him, and would have made Rebecca furious, he knew, if she'd overheard. Thankfully, she hadn't.

And now Mrs Deutschkron…

'There's no need to worry,' she said firmly, with an emphatic German flair to her accent. 'I am here to countermand the rubbish I gave you yesterday. I will have the treatment, please! Can it commence soon? Please, tell me how it is to be managed!'

'You've changed your mind,' he clarified. One of the most crashingly superfluous statements he'd made in a while.

'I have,' she confirmed. 'And I am very sorry to have wasted your time.'

There was an unmistakable zest to her which had been entirely absent yesterday, and he leapt to the conclusion which should have been obvious—would have been, if he'd been thinking clearly at the moment—from the second she walked in.

'You've had some good news.'

'I have had some marvellous news,' she assured him. 'My daughter is getting married. About time! She is thirty-eight! And I am going to be at that wedding—and it is going to be a *proper* wedding, I have told them, which will take weeks and weeks to organise. No using my health as an excuse to rush off to the register office in a knee-length dress, thank you!'

She wasn't smiling as she said all this. It was clearly far too momentous and important for the frivolous indulgence of a grin. But her whole manner was electrifying in its determination and happiness.

The entire complexion of Marsh's morning changed, and he urged her to tell him the whole story as there was clearly a story to tell.

Mrs Deutschkron got comfortable in her chair. 'Well,' she began, then immediately interrupted herself, 'Why it is that a parent cannot be *told* these things, I don't know! But it appears that Marianne has been going out—what do they do these days? They don't go out! They stay in! with this gentleman for a year. She has not mentioned it to me, she says, because she "did not know where it was heading".'

Mrs Deutschkron shook her head, as if in her generation

there had never been any possibility of ambiguity on the issue.

'But she was upset with me yesterday,' she went on, 'for deciding against the treatment, and she tells Jonathan about it—his name is Jonathan—and he says to her, "Would it change her mind if we got married?" What sort of a proposal is this? I would have turned it down! Thankfully, my daughter didn't. She brings him round to meet me last night—about time—and the whole thing is arranged. I ask you!'

She threw out her hands helplessly, and Marshall had the best laugh he'd had in weeks.

'Wonderful!' he said.

'It's perfect,' his patient agreed. 'And if there's any hope that this treatment might keep me going until there is a grandchild on the way...'

'It might, Hilde,' he told her. 'It might, at that!'

More good news came later in the day. Joan Allyson phoned to report that she'd got the result of her biopsy. 'It was something called a fibroadenoma, apparently, and not a tumour,' she said. 'Nothing to worry about.'

'That's great, Joan!' he told her. 'I'm so glad!'

Joan had her first immunisation shots the following Monday, completed them as scheduled and had her wedding. Meanwhile, Mrs Deutschkron began her chemotherapy, which had been set at six cycles at one-month intervals, over the course of six months.

Important things were happening in the lives of the practice staff, as well as the patients. Rebecca had begun to feel her baby move, and was approaching the halfway point in her pregnancy. Grace had announced that she was pregnant as well, and was obviously thrilled about it. She had Marcus's full support this time, instead of the cloud of his deep ambivalence which had hung over her last thwarted pregnancy.

And Aimee's house sale had gone through successfully.

'I'm in Summer Hill now,' she told everyone quietly at a practice meeting in early October. 'My new address and phone number are on the staff contact sheet.'

Marshall waited until he was alone at the reception desk and looked it up, wondering about the move. Aimee had hardly said anything on the subject—not to him, or to anyone else in the practice that he knew of. He almost got the impression that the move hadn't been something she'd really wanted, which didn't make sense. Whose wishes and needs did she have to consider but her own?

On the staff contact sheet, he read, 'Aimee Hilliard, Unit 7/63, Croydon Street, Summer Hill.' Then he actually looked it up in his street directory at home that night. Croydon Street was a main road, not far from the train. Was she looking ahead to a time when she couldn't drive any more? That could be thirty years away! Surely she couldn't have turned her back on their relationship out of a conviction that she was too old for a second chance at love?

As always, when he thought about Aimee, it all came back to this. After nearly two months, he still had no idea why she'd rejected him. Was it an innate problem with the male ego, he wondered, that he had to keep looking for *reasons*? Surely it wasn't! He didn't think that he was an overly egotistical man.

There's a natural harmony between us, he thought frequently. I can feel it.

He had plenty of opportunities to do so, working beneath the same roof with Aimee for approximately forty hours each week, exchanging small talk with her a dozen times a day, working in close partnership at times, too.

Just to pick one random scene out of their working lives as an example—removing two large moles from Maria Costanzo's left armpit and beneath her breast last week. Mrs Costanzo had made a nervous patient, and Marshall had half expected her to chicken out of the procedure at the last minute.

It hadn't been life-saving surgery. The moles had given every indication of being benign, but both of them had been positioned right at sixty-two-year-old Mrs Costanzo's bra line and they'd been large enough to become chafed and irritated by the constant contact. For any woman, it was a vulnerable area.

Aimee had assisted him, and as usual she'd done an enormous amount to reassure Mrs Costanzo and coax her into going through with the procedure.

'I think the moles are no worries after all. I live with it. It's not necessary to have the removal,' he'd heard his patient say in a frightened tone as he'd come to the door of the treatment room.

'Now, Mrs Costanzo, won't you be angry at yourself when you get home if you don't get it done?' Aimee chided her gently. 'You've already spent all that time being nervous. I bet you stayed awake half the night, didn't you?'

'Eh!' Mrs Costanzo said dismissively, then admitted, 'More than half!'

'So you've done the hard part!'

'The surgery, that's the hard part.'

'Believe me, it isn't! Being nervous before the surgery is harder!'

Aimee saw Marshall in the doorway and raised her eyebrows. Was he ready? He shook his head and made a gesture with his hand that said, Go on with what you're saying to her. She still looks as if she's about to bolt. Mrs Costanzo hadn't seen him yet, as she was lying on the table, facing away from the door.

'Now, why don't I just leave you alone for a moment to take off your upper clothing and then cover your torso with this sheet? Dr Irwin will be along in a minute. He'll tell you what he's going to do, and that's the point to change your mind if you really want to.'

Mrs Costanzo didn't change her mind, of course. Most nervous patients didn't, once they'd taken the step of getting undressed. During the procedure itself, Aimee remained in the room, chatting easily to the elderly woman and passing Marshall everything he needed with an efficiency that allowed him to make a seamless job of the surgery. Mrs Costanzo flinched at the painkilling injection, but Aimee encouraged her to turn her head in the opposite direction and close her eyes while Marshall made each incision.

The suturing was the worst part, but by then even the patient realised that there was no turning back. 'Oh, I can feel it!' she said in a panicky voice.

'The pain?' Aimee asked.

'No, the tweaking.'

'You're squeamish, I know. Tell me about that grandson of yours!'

'Oh, he's so naughty! He's going to wear me out! I have him two days a week now. But he's so cute!'

'All finished, Mrs Costanzo,' Marshall was able to tell her a few minutes later. 'Aimee will put on the dressings for you, and give you some instructions about how to look after the area and what to watch out for.'

As he left the room, he just had time to hear Aimee teasing, 'Now, tell me, which was worse? Having it done, or thinking about having it done?'

'The thinking. You were right,' Mrs Costanzo said.

Back in his own office, Marshall knew that he'd have been happy about getting such a good nurse for his practice even without any question of a personal attraction on his part. As things stood, he risked losing this valuable member of staff because he couldn't resolve what he felt.

Despite the harmony between them, she sometimes looked hunted in his presence, and she would often go out of her way to minimise the time they needed to spend together. It seemed wrong that she'd turned deliberately away from him at a time when she'd needed his support on the issue of her daughter's troubled pregnancy.

Even so, this was the subject on which they connected best. The pregnancy was hanging by a thread. Labour hadn't been triggered by that first drain, but now everyone in the practice knew that a second one was looming.

'She's having another ultrasound this morning,' Aimee reported to Deirdre at the front desk on the first Thursday in October, just before the day's first patients arrived.

Aimee had spent a sleepless night. After less than a week in her new home, she hadn't yet got used to the traffic noise on Croydon Street, but felt claustrophobic and cramped in the small second-floor flat if she slept with the windows closed. After thinking about her daughter and the baby half the night, she'd risen early, breakfasted quickly and fled the flat.

Opening up the practice and enjoying its welcoming decor and uncluttered rooms, she'd made a mental note to herself to be ruthless about the furniture and boxes still piled in each room. Would Sarah like any of her superfluous things? Or William?

Or perhaps, if I keep on looking, I can find something better, she thought. Further out, in a cheaper suburb. Two bedrooms, instead of one. Sydney prices were insane, and her credit-card statements still looked horrendous.

On a positive note, Sarah and Jason had been able to renegotiate their mortgage, which had, blessedly, dissolved away one of the sources of tension from Sarah's face. She would be able to afford to stay home with the baby for as long as she wanted to now, and this was becoming more and more important to her and to Jason as the likelihood of a problem with the baby increased.

'Dr Gaines is planning to drain off the fluid again,' Aimee continued to Deirdre. 'She's like a balloon. Tight as a drum and horribly uncomfortable.'

'How far along is she now?' Deirdre asked.

Aimee could see Marshall hovering in the background, looking at a file. She knew he was listening, and felt angry, though she recognised that this was illogical. It helped that he knew about this. She wanted him to know. And it was her fault that he didn't feel comfortable about asking her openly for news, and that she didn't have the right to seek all the comfort she wanted from him.

'Thirty-seven weeks,' she answered Deirdre, aware of Marshall abandoning his pretence of consulting the file as he approached to listen frankly.

Much better! There was quite enough painful pretence between them already!

'Which is fine if the baby's normal,' she said, 'but if it does have an incomplete oesophagus...if she needs surgery...'

'Would you like the day off?' Marshall offered, and Aimee turned on him.

'No!' she exclaimed abruptly. 'Thank you!' she went on in a jerky tone as she tried in vain to control herself. 'You've offered that before. But it wouldn't help. Haven't I already said that? There's nothing I can do. Sarah doesn't need me to hang around the hospital. Please, don't keep suggesting it, Marshall!'

'All right, I won't,' he said with quiet dignity. 'But the offer stands, Aimee. We'll manage. Any time you need to go to her.'

Aimee nodded, and managed another stiff, 'Thank you.'

She was hot all over, and knew she'd behaved terribly, and in front of Deirdre, too! She could only be thankful that Rebecca wasn't around, because the two of them got more awkward with each other as every day went by, although both sincerely tried not to be.

Rebecca's pregnancy had begun to show, but she was tall enough that there was plenty of room in there, so her bump was neat and taut and unobtrusive. She had just started to wear a repertoire of deliciously flattering maternity outfits, cleverly designed so that many people wouldn't have realised she was pregnant at all.

Aimee had never before experienced the shameful torment of being jealous of someone's good fortune, and she battled against feeling it now, but not always with success. Rebecca was positively breezing, floating, dancing through her pregnancy, and it wasn't fair that the case should be so different for Sarah, who'd scarcely got rid of her unrelenting and violent morning sickness, and hadn't shaken off her fatigue at all, before the sensation of bloating and discomfort had taken hold. Now there remained this horrible cloud over the baby's health.

'Want some tea?' Deirdre offered, just as Rebecca herself came through the front door. She was singing.

'Yes, please,' Aimee answered quickly.

'Morning, all!' Rebecca carolled blithely, and Aimee had to struggle to give a cheery greeting in reply.

She heard from Jason about an hour later, when the practice was humming along with its morning routine.

'The amniotic fluid index was sky high. They did the drain. Just over three litres,' he reported, 'but she's having some strong contractions.' He sounded strained and exhausted. 'The drugs don't seem to be helping, and they're getting concerned that they won't be able to stop it.'

'Is that OK?' Aimee asked uselessly. 'I mean, what have they said? Is it Dr Gaines?'

'He's been in and out. There's nurses. I'm losing track. Sarah's handling it OK. Just going by her state, I'd say it's going to happen.'

'OK. OK,' Aimee breathed. The word, repeated by both of them, was nonsense. Nothing was OK!

This is my daughter. I've done it myself. I've given birth three times. What was it like? I can't remember any more. And I never had this cloud...

'I need to get back to her,' Jason said. 'She reckons it hurts worse when I'm not there.'

'Oh, it does! I remember that!'

Aimee had been in the first generation of mothers to have their husbands present during labour and delivery, and suddenly the memories returned. Alan's hand in hers. His words of encouragement. He'd been ill at ease, not sure about his role. He hadn't always said the right thing, but his presence had helped enormously all the same, and she knew that Jason would do a wonderful job with Sarah.

'Go, then, Jason,' she told him. 'Give her all my love.'

'You still won't leave, will you?' Marshall said softly to her when he found her hiding in the treatment room between patients an hour later, her hands fluttering and her breathing shallow.

'No,' she answered, 'but I'm going to phone the hospital.'

She felt his arm fall lightly onto her shoulder. It had just begun to warm her through the fabric of her blue-green linen blouse when he let its weight rest there fully. He'd been giving her time, she knew, to shrug her way out of the contact if she didn't want it.

But, oh, she did! She wanted it so badly!

It had been weeks since he had touched her deliberately, and even the handful of times when it had happened by accident had obviously been occasions he'd tried to avoid by keeping his distance. A couple of times her skirt had brushed his trousers in the corridor. She'd felt his shoulder nudge her side as he'd sat at the front desk, scanning some notes, while she reached past him for a file. Once they'd bumped into each other in a doorway, and his hands had shot out in a reflexive gesture to steady them both by holding her upper arms.

Now she let herself lean into him, amazed at how familiar and right he still felt, despite all the awkwardness she'd thrown up between them. Standing behind her, he enclosed her in his arms, her head pressed back against his chest and his forearms beneath her breasts, her back and thighs warmed by the full length of him, and it wasn't until she felt his lips press the top of her head that she knew how unfair this was to both of them, and that she had to end it.

'I must make the phone call,' she gasped, and twisted out of his arms.

'Tell me the news,' he urged her stiffly. 'You know...how much I care, Aimee.'

She nodded, unconsciously closing her eyes, and wilfully misunderstood his words. 'The whole practice cares,' she answered him. 'And that helps.'

Phoning the hospital, she was transferred twice before she reached the right person and heard, 'Still not sure what's happening. Strong, irregular contractions. They may settle down.'

It was reassuring enough to allow her to get on with her

work, and she didn't hear any more until nearly three o'clock, when Jason rang again to gabble, 'It's not stopping. It's happening. Only a minute between contractions now, and she's seven centimetres dilated. I can't think.'

'I'll come straight to the hospital after work,' she promised urgently, but he'd already put down the phone.

'Aimee, why don't you go now?' Rebecca said gently, having overheard the promise and understanding the urgency in Aimee's tone.

'If just *one* more person says that to me, just one more time!' she threatened darkly in reply, her voice high and strident. Then she bit her lip.

Damn! Damn! Damn! Rebecca was really trying to be nice. I could hear the care in her voice, and I blew it!

'I'm sorry, Rebecca, I really am. That was completely uncalled for.'

'Hey...' The younger woman touched her arm, and Aimee was astonished to see tears in her eyes. 'Please, don't apologise! We all know what's going on. You must be a mess, and I think it's incredible that you're here at all, and carrying on in your usual calm, efficient and pleasant way.'

'Oh, Rebecca...'

Rebecca sniffed and had to pull a tissue from the box on the front desk. 'Hormones!' she said. 'Sorry. I'm thinking about that tiny girl!'

'Perhaps I'll just take Mrs Morgan's blood, and then head off,' Aimee conceded, moved by Rebecca's empathy when things were so awkward between them.

'Do that,' Rebecca agreed. 'And phone someone...Dad, I guess,' she suggested uncertaintly, 'when there's some news.'

'Uh-huh.' Aimee nodded.

She took the blood and prepared it for sending out to the

pathology lab in a state of shaky determination to stay focused, then left at a quarter past three and reached Southshore Hospital several minutes later.

A nurse at the entrance to the labour and delivery ward reported, 'She's very, very close. There'll be some news soon.'

Fifteen minutes after that, Jason appeared to report with a mixture of exultation and tears, 'She's born. She's beautiful. Little. She weighs two kilos. What's that? About four and a half pounds? We're calling her Bonnie Louise. They've taken her away to check her.'

He disappeared again, and Aimee allowed a passing nurse to persuade her in the direction of a cup of tea, though she drank only a sip of it. Then Jason was back.

'They've confirmed the diagnosis,' he said. 'Oesophageal atresia and a trackeo-oesophageal fistula.'

This had been an expected part of the condition—an opening between the lower pouch of the incomplete oesophagus and the windpipe leading to the lungs—but Aimee had been praying for better news. She knew how dangerous it could be, and wondered how much detail Jason and Sarah had been given. Stomach acid could flood upwards past the weak valve at the base of the oesophagus, through the hole and into the lungs, where it could critically damage the delicate new lung tissue.

'They're going to operate within the next few hours,' Jason finished.

It was the news they'd been expecting for two months, but that didn't make the reality of it any easier. Permitted to see the baby briefly before her journey down to the paediatric unit, Aimee was appalled at how small Bonnie Louise seemed. How could she possibly survive such dramatic, invasive surgery?

Aimee had never liked surgery. She had memories—they

seemed ominous now—of her stint in Theatres during her training over thirty years ago. Short-tempered surgeons, formidable nurses, rigid protocols and the drama of cutting and blood, monitors, respirators and tension stretched like high-voltage wires throughout the room.

Some things, she knew, had changed in thirty years. Tiny Bonnie's chances of survival and long-term health were vastly improved, and that was the most important difference. But the essential drama was the same. The baby was tiny, the surgery was her only chance of survival and every variable was critical.

Aimee had to battle to keep her mood high when she was allowed in to see Sarah, who was still in a state of postpartum triumph.

'She's gorgeous! And she had a great cry, Mum! Really strong! They say that's good. And I did it without drugs. I didn't want anything that might depress her system. Have you seen her yet?'

'Yes, she's beautiful.'

'And strong, don't you think?'

'Oh, strong, yes.' In spirit, maybe. Perhaps Sarah was perceiving this with a mother's instinct. Aimee hoped so.

The next few hours were a blur, filled with random scenes that would stay in her memory for ever. There was the maze of clean, bright hospital corridors. There was Sarah, transferred to a single room and starting to come down from her postpartum high as she focused on what lay ahead.

Aimee blessed the nursing staff for their sensitivity in allowing her daughter a room to herself when a good percentage of the rooms here were doubles. The last thing Sarah needed was the sight of another woman happily enjoying her healthy, normal baby.

Sarah was tired, still bleeding quite heavily, impatient

for a shower. She'd wanted to see Bonnie once more before the surgery, but Dr Gaines had persuaded her that it would be better to wait and concentrate on her own recovery.

'She'll need you to be strong and rested later on.'

Then there was Jason, trying to be the strong one, trying to remember every word the doctors told him and every movement the nurses made over baby Bonnie, trying to ask all the right questions so he could report it all back to Sarah. Aimee ached for him as she'd have ached if he'd been her own son.

His parents were overseas at the moment, sorting out Jason's elderly grandfather's living circumstances in Scotland, and he must have felt their absence as they were a nice couple and he was close to them.

There were the faces of the staff, unfamiliar, uniform in their concern and helpfulness, trying their very best.

And, finally, there was Bonnie. Aimee was able to see her twice more before she disappeared into surgery at seven. Each time they were mere glimpses, and each time Bonnie seemed more distanced by the frightening technology of modern medicine.

Already prepared for her journey to the operating theatre, she was in a special warmer with its own heating and was almost lost amongst the wires of three monitors, one on her hand and two on her chest. Also, there was the gold disc of a heat sensor on her stomach, a drip in her arm and a suction tube in her mouth.

Aimee stood helplessly by as Jason listened to explanations from the anaesthesia registrar, James Butler, and the surgeon, Denny Rutherford. There were X-rays to look at, suggesting that there was a second blockage at the exit from the stomach, but this wouldn't be known for certain until later on.

Jason nodded at Dr Rutherford's explanation, but Aimee

could tell he was just going through the motions. You had to be an expert to really see the problem on those grainy grey and white and blue-black films.

When Bonnie was wheeled away, Jason said at once, 'I'm going back to Sarah.'

Aimee decided aloud, 'I'll go home, I think, Jase. She won't be out of surgery for at least two hours, will she?'

'That's what they've said.'

'I'll come back then. Don't forget to eat, love.'

Her heart was heavy with empathy and she wanted to stay, but knew that he and Sarah needed some time alone more than they needed her hovering about.

Leaving the hospital in body, however, it didn't mean that she was leaving it in spirit. Her final glimpse of Bonnie haunted her and she felt exhausted and balanced on a knife-edge of fear. Her nursing experience was a curse, not a blessing, today. She'd seen ill newborns before, and had suffered through their pain, but this was her own grandchild, Sarah's first baby…

She drove for some minutes without consciously thinking about what she was doing. Driving was one of those things that came to be automatic after so many years of it, and she knew her way around Sydney like the native Sydneysider she was.

Then, ahead of her, a small yellow car darted out of a parking space at the side of the road and she slammed on her brakes. She came to a jarring halt less than a metre before contact, but the yellow car simply roared off without so much as a wave of apology from its driver.

Shakily, Aimee pushed on the accelerator once more, rather shocked by the incident, despite its harmless outcome. That had been her own fault as much as the other driver's. She'd better pay more attention to the road.

The road…

Now she suddenly felt sick as she took in her surroundings properly for the first time. This wasn't the route from Southshore Hospital to Summer Hill. This was Marshall's street, a short cut she'd often taken from Anzac Parade through to Woollahra, skirting the edge of Centennial Park.

But she didn't live in Woollahra any more.

After a cursory glance in her rear-view mirror, she pulled into a parking space, too upset to go on. She'd come miles out of her way, it was almost dark and she'd done this stupid thing! What on earth did that say about her state of mind, and about her feelings towards her new home? She shouldn't be driving in this state.

Needing to walk and to breathe deeply for a few minutes in order to settle herself, Aimee got out of the car and crossed to the park, aware of Marshall's house so close by. It was only a hundred metres or so ahead, just around a bend. It would be so good to see him, but that wasn't what either of them needed. Not when she was feeling like this.

But fate didn't seem to care about what was good for either of them today. Aimee saw him just a minute later, evidently returning from his evening jog through the park and heading for the pedestrian entrance just metres from where she stood as she tried to bring her breathing and her emotions back under control.

He didn't see her at first, and she debated the possibility of running away from the encounter, turning tail across the street and hiding in her car until he'd safely reached his house. She decided against it at the same moment that he caught sight of her, and had just enough time to calm herself a little before he slowed to a stop in front of her, his breathing heavy and his expression eager and concerned.

Before he could reach the wrong conclusion, she jumped in, 'I'm so silly, Marsh. I came the wrong way. Pure habit. Like a horse at a bad riding school, or something.' She tried to laugh, but it sounded more like a hysterical hiccup. 'Then when I realised, I got so jittery about it I had to stop. What an utterly foolish thing to do!'

Again she laughed, a high-pitched trill to her own ears.

Marshall was frowning, his hands on his hips and his head thrown slightly back as he attempted to slow his breathing.

'No, I'm the fool,' he said slowly, between heaving breaths. 'For a moment I thought you'd actually come because you needed to, because you couldn't help it. You needed someone to talk to about Sarah and the baby, and I was the person it had to be. But I should have known better. Lord knows, it'd be too much to expect that you'd actually get over whatever fear it is that's stopping you from accepting what we could have together. Clearly, in your case it's not a self-limiting illness, and if there's a cure, I don't have it!'

He turned from her, leaning his hands on his knees, still cooling off from what must have been an extended run tonight.

Aimee struggled for a moment before trying to speak. 'Marshall, I—'

'No, don't say anything.' He wheeled around again. 'I'm sorry. That was unforgivable. All of it.'

'Of course it wasn't. No, of course it wasn't, Marsh!' she repeated insistently.

They stood there, looking helplessly at each other. It was getting darker by the minute and she couldn't see his face nearly as well as she wanted to. He'd been angry a moment ago. Was he still?

The connection between them was so strong it was all she could do not to touch him. She felt as if she were suddenly blind, and the only way she could communicate or understand was the way a blind person would have, through touch. If she touched him, held him, felt his arms around her and the movement of his breathing, his mouth closing over hers, then she'd—

What? Nothing was in doubt, was it? She knew how she felt about him, and how much more she could feel if she let herself. She knew she'd hurt him, too, which told her how he felt towards her.

Who was it who had once said that you only hurt those you loved? Or had it been those who loved you? She couldn't remember. Maybe she'd made it up!

And anyway, the issue of what they each felt wasn't in question. It was the complexity of their lives—hers, in particular—that lay between them.

'I'm sorry, Aimee,' he said again. 'I've no right to bring any of this up now, and in such a way. Let's agree that you acted somewhat irrationally, and that you had every right to! Please, come in for a while, and tell me about Sarah and the baby.'

'Can I?' she asked him starkly. 'I—I think I need to. If you mean it…'

'Oh, believe me, I mean it!' Marshall said.

CHAPTER SEVEN

'HAVE you eaten yet?' Marshall asked Aimee once they were inside.

'No,' she answered. 'I told Jason to, but then I...' She laughed, and shook her head. 'I wasn't hungry at all before, but now I am. I haven't eaten all day.'

'We'll order Chinese, home delivery,' he decreed, and she felt no desire to argue.

So much for independence! She was in no hurry to find herself alone back at Summer Hill.

'Tell me what happened,' Marshall said.

He was opening a bottle of red wine, and he had two glasses waiting, but she shook her head, thinking of the drive back to the hospital later on. She was in such a state already, and didn't want anything that would impair her concentration at the wheel. Instead, she accepted some fruit juice mixed with sparkling mineral water, and sipped it as she told Marsh the news on little Bonnie.

'Who's her surgeon?' he asked, after listening to her account.

'Denny Rutherford is his name. He seemed young.'

'Oh, a baby!' Marshall teased. 'About forty, I think.'

She laughed. 'You're right. I'm showing my age.'

'You hardly ever do, Aimee. But, seriously, she couldn't be in better hands. He must have done that operation many times, both here and overseas, and not always under the best of conditions, so I doubt if anything could throw him off stride. I know quite a bit about him through Gareth

Searle at Southshore Health Centre, and I've met him twice.'

'That's all good to know. And I liked his manner. I think Jason was reassured.'

'Are you going to go back there tonight?'

'I'd like to.'

'Stay here until it's time and I'll drive you, then drop you home. We can work out something with your car tomorrow,' he promised vaguely.

But Aimee shook her head. 'I'll stay a couple of hours—thanks for suggesting it—but I'll go to the hospital by myself, Marsh.'

Under the cover of riffling through his selection of take-away restaurant menus, Marshall studied her and decided not to argue the point, although he would dearly have liked to. It was absurd, the way he felt, a complex, bubbling recipe of different emotional ingredients.

First, sheer exultation that Aimee was beneath his roof once more after two long months, and a determination to crowd the next three hours—she'd said two, but he wanted her here longer—with as many good things as he could think of.

Second, the prickling pain of knowing that nothing had really changed. She'd turned to him out of need and chance, and if he made the mistake of challenging her in any way, forcing her to acknowledge aloud what they both understood about their chemistry and their intuitive response to each other, he knew she'd close up like an echidna warding off its enemies by showing its spines.

Third, he simply wanted to look after her. He had an inkling that she wouldn't like that. Thinking back on all their dealings with each other, as he frequently did, he'd remembered several times when she'd been gently insistent on making her own decisions, doing things on her own—

tackling a difficult ski run on their weekend away, ordering her meal at a restaurant without advice from either the waiter or her dinner partner, locking up the practice at the end of a busy day.

'No, thanks. I can handle it on my own.' Firm, friendly, smiling. There was never a sting in it, always a light note of satisfaction, as if she wasn't quite accustomed to this independence and self-reliance and was just beginning to decide that she liked it.

Marshall had started to wonder about her marriage, and if that could be the source of her reluctance to become involved with a man again.

Had it been unhappy? Had Alan Hilliard been a domineering autocrat? Marshall didn't know, and wasn't inclined to ask straight out, but he decided to act on that assumption tonight and from now on, and felt, as he tasted the berry-rich wine on his tongue, more optimistic about Aimee than he had since the beginning of August.

Perhaps he'd been wrong to think that because they had no marriage, no actual commitment, it wasn't possible to work on the problem that was keeping them apart. Perhaps it was simply a question of taking things more slowly, being more prepared to feel his way.

He found the take-away menu he was looking for and they looked at it together, spreading it out on the coffee-table in front of the comfortably aged three-seater floral couch where they were sitting.

'Definitely prawns,' she decreed.

'You like prawns?' It was the most gentle of probes.

'Don't you?' She looked up, and he saw her getting ready to politely back down.

'No, I love them,' he said, 'but some people don't.'

'Alan didn't.'

Aha! 'Did that stop you?'

'Well…he felt they weren't safe.'

Aimee hadn't answered his question directly, but he didn't push the point, just felt another surge of the same satisfaction he'd experienced a few minutes earlier. He leaned a little closer to study the menu and could feel her warmth. He could have buried his face in her hair if he'd turned. It had started to come loose from its clip, and looked soft and smooth and silky, looping low across her ear.

'I fancy a soup to start,' he said, 'followed by something spicy. Beef, I think.'

They settled on a bean curd and vegetable dish as well, and Aimee said, 'You won't have to cook tomorrow either, because there'll be plenty left!'

After he'd ordered, he still felt that same impatient need to entertain her, take her mind off things, so he invited quickly, 'Come up and see my new bathroom.'

'Oh, is it finished at last?'

'Last week. I showered gloriously for twenty minutes as a celebration.'

'Spendthrift!'

'It's been a wet spring,' Marshall argued unrepentantly. 'The reservoirs are in good shape, and I had to test out the staying power of the new solar water-heater, didn't I?'

They were climbing the stairs as he spoke. He led the way along the corridor then stood back, watching her face as she took in the full symphony of white and green and gold. While retaining the character of the old house, he'd also gone for something opulent and luxurious.

'It's gorgeous!' Aimee said, then accused teasingly, 'I thought you hated baths.'

'I know.' He grinned wryly. 'The tub is huge. It's not for me—it's in case I decide to sell up. I was assured most avidly that a tub of such sybaritic proportions was an essential these days.'

'Oh, they'll tell you anything, won't they?' she said with a laugh.

'You think I was conned?'

'No, because I'm sure you're right. How could any buyer resist this? Are you seriously thinking of selling?'

'Might,' he admitted.

His voice had gone gruff all of a sudden, Aimee noticed, wishing she hadn't asked. Then, to make it worse, he noticed her regret.

'It's not a sore point, Aimee,' he said. 'But, let's face it, the house is too big for one man, and perhaps it's time I moved on. A little place on the coast, up on a cliff, a nice, quiet country practice with lots of retirees for patients.'

'You mean, not just leaving this house but leaving the practice and Sydney?' The idea was too unexpected to allow her to hide her shock. And yet perhaps it would be better for both of them if he did go away.

His glance was quizzical. 'People make changes,' he said. 'You've just made a big one yourself, and presumably for similar reasons.'

'I— Oh, yes,' she interrupted herself quickly. 'Much less work to look after something small. I'll be able to get it just as I want it, then have much more spare time for other things. Helping Sarah, or going away. Thomas has always promised me he'd take me on a field trip some time, and show me some of his beloved creatures.'

It all started to make sense as she said it, and for the first time since Peter's news over two months ago she felt as if she was getting back in control, able to mould the clay of the life she'd been given as she wanted to.

If I can't afford to live in a place I love, then I'll simply find better things to do than being at home! she decided. I am *not* going to let any of this defeat me!

They talked a little more about their children. Marshall was looking forward to a visit to Simon in the United States at Christmas. Aimee was a little concerned that William would choose a career in administration or business because of the security it offered, not because it was what he really wanted. He'd always been very good with children, and she'd have liked to see him go into primary-school teaching, where he could be of real value and where she was sure he would be much happier. Neither of them mentioned Rebecca.

Then the doorbell rang. It was their meal, which they hadn't yet set the table for.

'Or shall we eat in front of the box?' Marshall suggested. 'I have a couple of videos we could watch. Both comedies,' he added, as an extra inducement.

It worked. 'Probably just what I need,' Aimee confessed.

'I thought it might be,' Marshall responded, and she didn't miss the note of quiet satisfaction in his voice.

Was it cowardly of her not to examine too closely what that satisfaction might mean?

Together, they brought plates, cutlery, napkins and glasses to the glass-topped coffee-table, then Marshall put on the movie, which made the time pass quickly and took Aimee's mind off Bonnie's surgery.

Not that anything could do that fully tonight. Her thoughts travelled frequently to her new little granddaughter, only to be dragged mercifully back to what was happening on the screen.

Beside her, Marshall ate heartily and laughed his rich, frank laugh, which both warmed and soothed her. They didn't talk much, but when they did it felt good. He poured her a little more mineral water, which he was now also drinking himself, and paused the movie halfway through to suggest coffee.

Aimee nodded. 'I might be up late. I wouldn't mind the caffeine.'

'Don't think that I'm not thinking about her as well,' he told her.

'I know, and I'm glad now about that silly mistake earlier, driving home to Woollahra.'

'So am I.'

She helped him make the coffee, despite his insistence that she shouldn't and as they stood together in the kitchen it would have been so easy to seek out the sensual support of his touch. Those knotty, sensitive hands of his holding her, his forehead hard against her face as he whispered just the right words.

She pushed the need away, and thought about the coffee instead, smelling the rich aroma as he ground beans in an electric grinder, then put them into a tiny cappuccino-maker. Aimee was impressed by it, and said so.

'Oh, we're very European here.' He laughed. 'Rebecca gave it to me for Christmas a couple of years ago, and I wish I had as good an excuse as this to use it more often.'

The words created their own silence, and she couldn't think of a safe reply. All she could do was murmur inanely after a few moments, 'Mmm, the smell!'

This time he was the one who didn't answer.

As soon as the movie was over Aimee told Marshall, 'I must get back to the hospital. Bonnie will be out of surgery by now.'

Just saying it aloud was enough to make her feel shaky and upset again, and when Marshall repeated his offer to drive her there she didn't turn him down. His companionship and support would be so nice tonight, had been so nice for almost three hours already. She'd arrived here at about seven, and it was now almost ten.

'I'll take you home afterwards, too,' he promised easily.

At that, she froze inside but managed not to let it show, and excused herself to the bathroom, purely to buy some time. She didn't want him to see her new home, the tiny flat in the ugly red-brick building, separated from a noisy main road by just a few metres of pale concrete pavement. It would jar completely with his expectations of the kind of place she'd have chosen. What had possessed her to agree to let him drive her? She hadn't been thinking properly. Thinking with her heart, not her head.

When Aimee came down from the bathroom again, she told him too brightly, 'I've been thinking…' If only I'd done it sooner! 'It really doesn't make sense for you to take me, and create all that nuisance about my car. I'll be fine, really I will.'

She could hardly have missed the sudden sharp glance that shot her way, or the short but telling pause before he spoke.

'I really don't mind, Aimee. I'd like to be there. It's ridiculous to make a fuss about the car. We can take yours, and I'll get a taxi back from your place.'

Stupidly, she spoke her immediate thought aloud. 'That's a very practical solution, but—'

'But it doesn't address the real problem, does it?' he finished for her.

They were standing in the wide front hallway, and he was watching her, reading her. He wore his metal-framed glasses low on his nose so that they looked rakish and endearingly human. Yet 'endearing' wasn't really the right word in the current context. Far too staid. Aimee didn't feel that Marshall was dear, she felt he was devastating and dangerous and she wanted him so badly that it shocked her to the core.

This? She had the capacity to feel *this*? So churned up, so sizzlingly sensitive in every nerve ending, so hungry, physically, for his touch. For the first time it struck her that he was still wearing his jogging clothes—a white knit shirt with a soft collar and black shorts in a rather stiff synthetic fabric. Why hadn't he changed?

Because he hadn't thought of it. They'd both been too consumed with the simple fact of being together, talking, reading each other's silences, thinking about the baby.

'No, it doesn't,' she answered his telling observation at last.

He went on, spelling it out for both of them. 'Because the real problem is that you're terrified of what we feel for each other for some reason.'

'I'm not,' she denied, and it was partly the truth.

Only partly, and he didn't accept it. 'For heaven's sake, Aimee, whatever else you're determined to deny me, don't, at least, deny me the chance to talk about it openly. For two months, we've both tried to pretend that we'd forgotten what we started, but we haven't, have we? It's still there, stronger than ever, and I don't understand what scares you so, why you're denying it and hiding from it.'

'I— It's...' She searched desperately for something, other than the truth, that would satisfy him. But, of course, it didn't work. He knew too much about people, and too much about her.

'Don't!' His voice was low, and vibrated with emotion. 'Just don't! If you can't, or won't, tell me the truth, then don't say anything at all.'

He stepped closer. Close enough to touch. He reached out a hand and let his fingers fall gently on her neck, tracing its warm contours, trailing up to her jawline and back into her hair, which had almost fallen completely from its clip at the back. He didn't speak.

Another step brought him close to take her in his arms, but he didn't. Instead, he simply dropped his hand and touched his mouth to hers. No other contact between them, just that. The kiss was slow, slow, the pressure of his lips feather-light at first as her chin lifted instinctively to meet them. He was giving her every opportunity to turn away, to say or signal her rejection of him, but she couldn't do it.

Aimee kept her eyes open and saw his gaze boring into hers across the glinting barrier of his glasses, then he turned aside for just long enough to reach up and remove them. It was a very deliberate gesture, as if he was saying, there! I'm naked now, and I dare you to try and lie to me when I've stripped myself for you!

He deepened his kiss, his hands on her shoulders and his body pressing against her so that they could both feel every contour—the places where they clashed, and the places where they could have joined, as they'd joined once before.

Now, at last, he spoke, taking his mouth from hers as it formed each phrase, then swooping back to claim her once more.

'Let me see,' he said. 'What are all the possibilities I've considered? That you don't want me? I think we can cross that one off the list.' His mouth made a trail down her throat and paused to kiss the hollow at the base of it.

'Marshall…!'

'That you made a vow of some kind to Alan?' He sighed. 'Surely it can't be that! It's too Victorian! Could you have stayed married for twenty-six years to a man who would have asked that of you? And if you'd given such a vow freely, because you knew you could never love another man as much, surely you wouldn't have let yourself respond to me as you did at first, so freely and happily. No, it's not that!'

He ploughed on, almost cruel in his insistence on saying it all, but kissing the cruelty away with lips that were utterly tender.

'Are you afraid then?' he suggested. 'Was your marriage to Alan miserable, and you can't imagine that I could make you happy as time went on? I could, Aimee!'

'I know…' The ragged confession was torn from her as his hands slid up her sides to touch her breasts through the soft linen of her blouse.

'Then perhaps it's that you're too lazy. Because, of course, it would take work. There would be a lot of decisions to make, other people to consider and convince. But I didn't think you were a lazy person, Aimee.'

'This isn't fair!' she gasped, dragging herself from his arms at last. 'It isn't fair at all, Marsh! What do you want from me? I was wrong to turn to you tonight. I wouldn't have if I hadn't made that stupid mistake and found myself in your street. I was praying that I wouldn't see you. Oh, I suppose it's my fault for giving in to you. I hoped you'd respect…respect the boundaries we'd both put in place. Please, respect them!'

'When you won't give me any sort of a reason to?' he demanded, unrepentant and angry now.

'I can't! Give me time!'

'How much?'

'I don't know.'

She let the familiar thoughts tumble helter-skelter through her mind. In time, when she'd made her new flat as nice as she could, worked out whether she was managing to save…

No. She'd never regain the sense of equality she'd had with him before Peter's news, and before she'd known about his inheritance. And Rebecca would always be on the scene as a reminder of the disparity between them, unsuccessfully trying to mask her suspicions and hostility, guarding her future legacy.

Perhaps if Marsh left Sydney, as he'd suggested he might, scaled down his life a little, but that possibility was too vague. There was nothing she could promise him.

'Yes, I do know,' she told him bluntly, contradicting her last uncertain words. 'It's not possible, Marshall. I won't deny the attraction between us… Well, it would be pointless, wouldn't it?' She laughed jerkily. Forgive me, Alan, I'm ignoring all the good years you gave me, taking advantage of your faults when I say this. 'But I didn't very much enjoy being married the first time, and I'm very much enjoying my independence now. I have no desire to relinquish that in exchange for the dubious advantages of being your wife—'

'I hadn't realised you were so militant in your feminism.'

She ignored him. 'And I imagine Rebecca, for one, would be very relieved to hear me say so.'

She closed her eyes and cursed the way her tongue had run ahead of her good sense. She hadn't meant to mention Rebecca and, of course, he didn't let it pass.

'Damn, is this about Rebecca? I know she's been—'

'It's not. It's not. She and I simply share our scepticism about this, that's all.'

He studied her, his eyes glittering and his hair standing wildly on end where he'd rubbed it with an agitated hand. 'This is a side of you I haven't seen, Aimee.'

'No?' She hugged her arms across her body. 'Are you surprised at it? You must have realised I didn't end what we had lightly, or without thought. We're not in our twenties, Marshall. That fact is so important! We're much wiser, thirty years on, and we're far more laden with baggage, all the baggage of two complicated lives. I don't believe, any more, that love conquers all, and I haven't got the energy at this point—' to her horror, she felt tears coming, beyond her control '—to keep arguing about it with you! I want to get to the hospital to see my daughter and her baby, Marsh. Please, accept that that's my priority.'

He nodded, and the fight went out of him, to be replaced by his usual concern. 'Of course. I'm sorry. This evening was supposed to help, wasn't it? But it hasn't, in the end.'

He sounded so bleak that she couldn't let it go by, and told him warmly, 'Oh, but it has helped! It did, until just now, enormously. I was too harsh.'

'And I was cruel.'

'Yes, you were.'

'I'm sorry. And now we've both apologised, I suppose that's all there is to say.'

'I think so.'

'Are you all right to drive?'

She had a tissue in her hand and was wiping her eyes. She had to be all right to drive, because she wasn't waiting there for a taxi! 'I'm fine.'

'Let Bev know if you can't come in tomorrow, and she'll arrange for an agency nurse.'

Aimee nodded and let him open the front door for her.

'Goodnight, Aimee.'

'Goodnight.'

By focusing intently on the roadway, Aimee reached the hospital with the knowledge that she'd driven safely. Then, in the main foyer, she ground to a sudden halt, not knowing where to go. Sarah's room? The recovery ward? The paediatric intensive care unit?

She asked a couple of helpless, incoherent questions at the desk, then waited for the woman on duty to phone through to the paediatric ward, feeling alone and drained and afraid that she would somehow let Sarah and Jason down tonight by not being half as strong as she wanted to be for them.

That scene with Marshall in his front hallway had drained her completely. She was devastated at the way he'd fought her, battling for his own vision of what they could have together. If he only knew how close he'd come to convincing her! The trouble was, her imagination was just as vivid as his, and it conjured up some very different scenes.

How would he handle a permanent breaking down of the closeness he had with his daughter, for example? Aimee knew how vital they'd been to each other thirteen years ago when Joy Irwin had been dying. She hated the thought of coming between them, especially when Rebecca was soon to give Marshall his first grandchild.

And how long would it take before her financial dependency on him turned into an emotional and practical dependency as well, in every aspect of their lives? The possibility was vivid and real, and she shuddered at the thought of repeating the pattern she'd had with Alan.

From the day of their marriage until just weeks before his death their bank accounts had been in his name only, and she'd never been able to spend a dollar without his approval. He'd given her a set amount for housekeeping each week, precisely calculated and precisely increased on occasion to keep pace with inflation, so that she was never left short but never had money left over to spend freely either.

He'd bought her clothing as gifts, or in the form of some cash pressed into her hand without warning and a decree, 'Buy yourself a dress.'

Twice she'd made the mistake of coming home with

something different—a woollen sweater once and the second time a pair of smart Italian leather shoes, which she'd wanted more than a dress, and he'd frowned. 'You shouldn't need shoes again this soon, should you? Navy? Did you really need navy shoes?'

'Would you like me to try and return—?'

'No, no, never mind.' He'd waved the offer aside with the sort of irritable indulgence he'd showed to the children when they'd squandered their small amount of pocket money unwisely.

It might have been easier now, perhaps, if Alan had been more deliberately cruel and autocratic about it, but he hadn't been. He had been, at heart, a kind man. He'd sincerely believed that a woman wanted to be treated that way, and he'd told her more than once, 'It makes me happy to be able to spoil you.'

He hadn't understood, and she'd never been able to get him to see, that he could have spoiled her occasionally without treating her on a day-to-day basis like a dependent child.

'We'll go to Surfer's Paradise for our holiday this year... I'm going to buy a new car... The children should get bikes for Christmas...' She'd never really been consulted, and the 'don't you think?' or 'if you agree' at the end of each announcement had been a mere formality. She hadn't known until after Alan's death quite how much she'd felt imprisoned by all that.

'I've rung P.I.C.U.,' said the woman at the desk, drawing Aimee's attention back to the present. 'Your granddaughter is there with her parents, and you can go up, but only for a short while.'

'Which—?'

'The fourth.' The older woman anticipated her question and gave her a sympathetic smile.

I must look as bad as I feel!

She took the lift, soothed just a little by the peaceful atmosphere of the hospital this late at night. There were few visitors about, and even fewer doctors. Most of the patients would be asleep, and all the non-urgent activities such as cleaning or physiotherapy wouldn't resume until normal working hours.

The double doors leading to the paediatric intensive care unit were closed, and Aimee had to press a buzzer to gain admittance. The unit consisted of eight beds, each in its own separate and generous-sized cubicle, with a central nursing station where every one of the unit's many monitors showed its reading in a single display.

Aimee saw Sarah first. She was dressed in one of her maternity outfits, a matched set of navy blue stretch leggings and a long A-line top, short-sleeved with a scooped curve of a neckline. Her dark blond hair was scraped back into the teeth of a big tortoiseshell clip, and her face looked clean and shiny and tired.

Jason stood beside her, and they were both helplessly rooted to the floor next to the baby's warming unit. A nurse was there, too, in the middle of answering what must have been a question from Sarah.

'From the tape they used on her skin in Theatre,' she said, only the words came out as 'teep' and 'skun' and 'therta', because she was a New Zealander with a strong accent which was soothing and pleasant.

'Hello, everyone!' Aimee said softly as she approached the group.

'Mum…' Sarah reached out her arms and laid her head on Aimee's shoulder.

'She's back.' No one minded that Aimee had stated the obvious.

'Only just,' Jason said. 'There was some delay before they could start. I don't know why.'

'A more urgent operation,' the New Zealand nurse, Sylvia, said.

'More urgent. Can't even imagine!' Jason commented weakly.

'How is she?' Covered in iodine stains and tubes and wires and dressings, still not fully emerged from the anaesthesia, but that wasn't what Aimee meant.

'We got a good report,' Jason said with an effort. 'The fistula has been closed. And the gap between the two pouches of the oesophagus wasn't too bad. Only a centimetre and a half. That's good, they reckon. The smaller, the better. Less chance of the join springing a leak, and of her needing further surgery for constriction of oesophagus later on.'

'What about the blockage in the duodenum?'

'They're going to wait on that. They'll be feeding her through an IV for a few days, then they'll do a test.'

'With dye?'

'That's right. It'll show up on a screen, and they'll be able to see if it keeps on going out of the stomach and into the intestines, or if it stops.'

'Mum,' Sarah said, 'I have to learn to express my milk.'

'I can try to help, if you need me.' Aimee had had some training in this area.

'They have a lactation nurse here. But once I'm discharged… We don't have any of the stuff. The pump and the bottles.'

'We'll work it all out,' Aimee soothed. 'I can phone around, go and buy things.'

They all stood there for some minutes more, just watching the baby, and Aimee heard Sarah murmur in a foggy voice, 'She's beautiful.'

She was too. Bonnie's fighting spirit, and her future promise most of all, but her little head, as well with its downy little cap of black hair, its tiny chin and nose, its high, square forehead and skin that was going to be creamy and fine-pored and fabulous when it wasn't rashy and red from the tape and yellow-stained from the iodine.

The scars on her chest, though they must be huge and raw at this stage, beneath the dressings that covered them, would eventually stretch and fade as Bonnie grew.

Aimee ached to touch her. She ached even more for Sarah and Jason, who were permitted the contact of a single hand but not yet the full joy of being able to cuddle her in their arms. How long would it be?

'What happens next?' Jason was asking the nurse, the helplessness in his voice an aching contrast to his manly build and his patent intelligence.

'Try and get some sleep, all of you,' Sylvia answered. 'That's what we want this little princess to do. She's had a big first day, and sleep is the best healer.'

They stayed a little longer, watching Bonnie begin to stir and grimace and startle, then Jason and Aimee accompanied Sarah back to her room.

'Want us to go or stay?' Jason asked his wife tenderly, kissing her forehead.

Lovely man!

Aimee felt another surge of emotion. Thank goodness my daughter is married to the right man!

'Go, I think,' Sarah answered him. 'I need to sleep. The nurse said it'll be hard to express milk if I'm stressed or fatigued or distracted.'

She gave a dry laugh, and neither Jason nor Aimee needed her to explain the reason for it. Just how on earth was she supposed to be unstressed and undistracted?

'Will we see you tomorrow, Mum?' she wanted to know.

'Of course. Not sure when, but as much as I can. Night-night, love.'

Aimee kissed Sarah and hugged Jason, then left him to say his own private goodnight, but he caught up to her at the lift and they walked to the car park together in silence, before parroting some more repetitive phrases to each other that couldn't begin to express the depth of what they felt.

Reaching home half an hour later, Aimee entered her new flat without even noticing its bland and slightly shabby paintwork, its ugly light fittings and the irritating hum of the fridge in the cramped kitchen. Did any of that really matter?

No! *No!* It was the people in her life who mattered. Sarah and Jason and the boys. Her parents in Queensland, whom she must phone first thing tomorrow with a full report on the day's events. Most of all, at the moment, the new being who had entered the world just today.

Would there ever be a safe place for Marshall in her heart as well? At the moment, she couldn't see it.

CHAPTER EIGHT

'SO OF course I just kicked myself for the rest of the day for changing my mind at the last minute. If I'd backed Sunset Raider instead of Galway Bound, I would have won over $1200 on the trifecta, though, of course, I did do quite well on Race Three with the quinella. Grape Juice and Falsetto, but they were the favourites so they didn't pay all that much. And the only thing that really cheered me up was the rugby. Are you a fan?'

'Of course,' Marshall answered gallantly, though he didn't live or die by sports results of any kind.

He was doing his best to find this new acquaintance fascinating and attractive, since he knew he was supposed to, but it was hard work. People shouldn't matchmake unless specifically asked to do so, he concluded. He liked his son-in-law Harry's parents, but would have enjoyed this Sunday barbecue at Rebecca's more if they hadn't brought divorced Diana Wetherill and introduced her in such a suspiciously casual way.

She was a perfectly pleasant person, in her early fifties with auburn hair and some comfortable but not over-abundant poundage settled on her hips, and there were many men who would have been delighted to find a woman so devoted to rugby and cricket and radio racing broadcasts, as well as regular flutters at the local betting agency. Unfortunately, he wasn't one of them.

'Another satay stick, Dad? Diana?' Rebecca asked.

'No, thanks, gypsy. I should be heading home soon, I

expect. On call. You know how it is,' he said in an aside to Diana. She nodded and smiled sympathetically.

Rebecca knew him too well to argue the point. She also knew perfectly well that he was simply making an excuse. His on-call at the practice could be covered just as well from Harry's and Rebecca's house in Surry Hills as it could from his own place just a few kilometres away.

In a city practice like this, most people went to the accident and emergency department at the hospital if they needed to be seen urgently. The two nursing homes covered by himself and his partners were the most likely sources of a call-out, as the elderly residents were frail, confused or infirm and didn't find it easy to travel.

'If you need to, Dad,' Rebecca told him lightly, then busied herself with offering barbecued satay sticks to the rest of her guests—Harry's parents, the young couple from the house next door and Harry's sister and her husband and two daughters.

Under cover of all the action, Marshall quietly left. He tipped a wink and a quick word of thanks to his son-in-law, then went through the house and out the front door.

His car was parked a little farther along the street, squeezed into a space that would take some manoeuvring to get out of. As he reached it he saw that the problem was even worse than he'd thought. A smaller car had left since he'd taken the space in front of it, and a larger car had squeezed in behind him instead, just fitting between his rear bumper and a driveway.

He sighed. It was hot in the street in the early afternoon sun, and he'd need help if he was going to get out without scraping one of the cars that had him so nicely sandwiched.

'Boxed in?' It was Rebecca, who must have followed him out of the house.

'Yes, did you already know?'

'No, that wasn't why I came out.'

He raised his eyebrows.

'Just checking that you were all right. Was Diana getting on your nerves?'

'No, she was fine. Would have been,' he amended more honestly, 'if I hadn't known I was expected to…to… You know.'

'Sorry. Rhonda's idea, not mine. I told her that—' She stopped, and began again. 'Well, I told her you weren't interested in any sort of—' Again she broke off, then accused heatedly, 'But Aimee's leaned on you a lot over the past couple of weeks since Bonnie's birth. Is it really so hopeless? I can't believe she's deliberately taking advantage of—'

'I don't know what she's doing,' Marshall heard himself admit. 'I wouldn't say she was leaning on me. She and her family have been through a huge ordeal with Bonnie. First there was the discovery that Bonnie did have the second blockage in her duodenum and needed surgery to correct that. Then the setback when she got an infection. Sarah's had a struggle to express enough milk, and then to get Bonnie to keep it down.'

'She has reflux because of a weak valve, I suppose.'

'Exactly. They're hoping now that she'll be discharged next week, but they're still not sure. Aimee's talked to me a lot about it. We've given her time off. But it's nothing special, Rebecca. I'm happy that she looks on me as a friend she can turn to, that's all.'

'Garbage, Dad,' Rebecca accused impatiently. 'That is not "all"! You want a hell of a lot more than that from her, and she's hurting you, and I can't stand to see it. It makes me so angry!'

She reached up to pat his shoulder, and the growing bump of her pregnancy nudged his lower stomach. She had passed the halfway point now, but hadn't yet reached the critical weeks when the baby would be just viable if born. Aware of the long-term health risks for very premature babies, as all doctors were, Rebecca was counting the days with extra tension until she reached the safer milestone of the third trimester.

'That isn't fair, Rebecca,' Marshall soothed her. 'Please, don't blame this on Aimee.'

'Oh, so who do you suggest I do blame it on?' Her frown was black, her colour high, and she was clearly spoiling for a battle.

'No one! There is no one at fault in this.' Instinctively, he wanted to protect Aimee, and Rebecca read him clearly at once.

'I can't stand this!' she stormed, pacing and punching at the air with her arms. 'That you care so much about her you won't even let me be angry with her. What is her problem that she can't see what a precious gift you're giving her? Why is she rejecting it? She doesn't deserve to have you feeling like this about her!'

'Rebecca—'

'I'm sorry. I don't suppose you need to hear this. I should keep my thoughts to myself on the subject, but it's been going on for months now—'

'I'll handle it, all right?' he told her, then managed a laugh. 'It's a little disconcerting to see my daughter attempting to mother me. Could you turn some of the maternal instinct of yours onto Harry, please, for the next four months or so?'

'This isn't just hormones, Dad!' she muttered darkly.

'Perhaps it's the heat, then,' Marshall suggested, determined to bring the subject to a close. 'Help me get out of this vehicular sandwich and go back inside for a long, cool drink.'

'Sure, if that's what you want.' She nodded stiffly.

And she claims it isn't hormones! he thought, then said slowly, 'Look, I'm— Yes, it's not easy.' His voice grew husky and he cleared his throat with some energy. 'I wish things had worked out differently. It's good to know that I have your support, but there's nothing to be gained by talking about it, gypsy, so, if you don't mind, we'll close the door on the whole thing, OK?'

'If that's what you want,' she repeated, but more softly this time. Then she stretched up and kissed his cheek.

His shoulders ached from wrestling with the steering-wheel by the time she'd guided him out of the tight parking space, and his shirt was stuck to his back with sweat before the car's air-conditioning dealt with the built-up heat inside. At home, he passed a lacklustre afternoon, filling in time with a bit of gardening and almost welcoming the call-out he received at four to Hazel Cleary Lodge, where a ninety-four-year-old patient had fallen and was refusing to accept the strong possibility of a broken hip.

The agony she experienced when he tried to help her to her bed— 'If I can just lie down for a little while, I'll be fine,' she'd said—finally convinced her that she needed hospital treatment, and she was taken away by ambulance.

This outcome had to count as a success, although realistically her long-term outlook wasn't brilliant, sustaining a fracture like that at her age.

'Independent to the end,' commented a caring member of the nursing-home staff. 'Good luck to her! I do think the fighters like her have the right idea.'

Marshall agreed, and went home feeling that he ought to be able to apply those words to his own life, but he didn't quite know how. Instead, he jogged. For miles.

* * *

'You didn't have to come in, Mrs Deutschkron. I would have been happy to come and see you at home,' Marshall told his patient.

'Ach!' she answered in her usual way. 'I wanted to get out. So sick of my walls!'

'And you're not feeling too good?'

'It didn't affect me so much the first time, but this time this—what do they call it? Cycle? It's really bad.'

'Yes, it can happen like that.' Marshall nodded.

'I am doing everything they told me at the hospital, but now there is this new thing, a feminine problem that is making me itch. I don't know if it is connected with the chemotherapy, but it is Marianne's and Jonathan's wedding on Saturday, and I don't want to be feeling this need that is not socially acceptable, all through the ceremony and the reception.'

'Of course not!' he said. 'The wedding is just three days away. It's on my calendar at home.'

Marshall had received a formal white and gold invitation for himself 'and guest', and had replied in the affirmative. Time passed too quickly, though. He hadn't yet asked his 'guest', which was a piece of inexcusable procrastination. He understood what lay behind it. Aimee was the guest he wanted to invite, but he'd been stalling, foolishly, waiting until the time seemed right. Now the date had caught up with him, and he'd left it too late.

The problem didn't concern Mrs Deutschkron, so he put it aside for the moment.

'It sounds like a yeast infection,' he told her. 'That's quite common in patients who are having chemotherapy. Your immune system isn't working as well as it should because of the treatment. I'll prescribe a cream and some pills.'

'More pills!'

'I know. Tedious. But it should do the trick by Saturday

and save you from embarrassment and discomfort. Hopefully the plan your oncologist has you on will help with the nausea by Saturday, too.'

'Yes, because I have foolishly chosen to wear a shade of pale green which at this point will rather too closely match the shade of my face!'

Mrs Deutschkron was looking noticeably thinner and weaker, though it was clear her spirit hadn't deserted her. She wore a smart trouser suit, as well as some very bright chunky jewellery and a big silk scarf folded into a triangle and knotted around her shoulders.

She'd come by taxi, she said, because Marianne was too busy with wedding preparations and work pressure to bring her, and she seemed quite content to contemplate returning home by the same means.

Marshall wasn't as enthusiastic. It was three in the afternoon, which was the shift change-over for Sydney taxi drivers, it was raining heavily and the wait even to get through on the phone to make a booking could be horrendous at such times. Also, Mrs Deutschkron needed to visit the chemist to get her two prescriptions filled.

'Our practice nurse will take you home, via the pharmacy,' Marshall promised Mrs Deutschkron, and the feeble brevity of her protest before she accepted the offer told him what an effort she was making to disguise how ill, weak and uncomfortable she felt.

'Wait in the waiting room,' he told the elderly woman. 'She'll be along in a minute.'

Ducking out of his office while Mrs Deutschkron gathered her bag and umbrella, he found Aimee in the treatment room, taking blood from a patient who was due for major surgery the following week.

'Lovely veins,' she was saying, her fingers gentle in the crook of Russell Cartwright's arm. He was a rugby player in his mid-twenties, hairy of leg and thick of neck, and he was as scared as a kitten, Marshall noticed as he hovered in the doorway.

Aimee had noticed, too. 'You would swear some people's veins actually hide when they see me coming,' she chatted on cheerfully and deliberately, and she had the needle inserted and the blood filling the syringe nicely before her patient even had time to wince and hiss. 'There, that's all we need,' she finished a few minutes later.

'You mean, that's it?' Russell questioned, as if he couldn't believe he'd got off so lightly.

'I can take some more if you think you've got too much of the stuff,' she teased.

This earned a hasty, 'No, thanks.' Then he lumbered off as fast as decently possible.

Aimee didn't say anything, just looked up at Marshall and waited to hear what he wanted. This was the way they most often seemed to communicate now. No words wasted. Reading each other effortlessly.

'All right if I get you to run Mrs Deutschkron home?'

'Of course.'

'Could you stop off at the pharmacy, too, on the way? I've prescribed her a couple of things for a yeast infection.'

'Feeling it this time?'

'Badly, if I'm any judge. The nausea, and now this infection. And the wedding's this Saturday.'

'Oh, what a shame!'

'I've been invited,' he told her abruptly, 'And guest. Meant to tell you weeks ago. Would you like to come?'

Aimee hesitated, then heard Rebecca's voice a little farther along the corridor. 'See you again next week, then, Mrs Colson.'

'Yes, I would,' she answered Marshall quickly. 'That would be lovely.'

Rebecca was following her patient towards the waiting room, and a quick acquiescence seemed like the safest way to change the subject.

But Marshall went on, 'It's at three. I'll pick you up.'

Rebecca passed by at that moment. She didn't say anything, and then Aimee and Marshall both heard the clatter and the little cry that came from his surgery.

He disappeared from the doorway, and she heard him ask, 'Are you all right, Mrs Deutschkron?'

'I have very stupidly dropped my umbrella.'

'I'll pick it up for you, Mrs Deutschkron,' Aimee said, and she stepped into the situation, retrieved the umbrella from beneath Mrs. Deutschkron's chair and helped the ill woman out of the surgery and along the corridor.

'I'll bring my car to the side entrance,' she went on, 'and Andrea will walk you out to meet me.'

It took half an hour to drive to the chemist's, get the prescription filled and deliver Mrs Deutschkron home, by which time the elderly lady was almost too exhausted to stand. Aimee phoned the practice to let them know that she would be absent longer than expected, then helped Mrs Deutschkron to bed. She was due for some tablets, so Aimee helped her take those, then prepared a can of soup and a cup of tea for her.

'I'll be better after a sleep,' Mrs Deutschkron insisted. 'And Marianne said she would be here at six.'

Two hours away. 'Is she staying the night?'

'She will if I ask her to.'

'Please, ask her to,' Aimee suggested firmly, and didn't receive a protest.

Back at the surgery, there was some good news on young Aaron Lloyd, the boy who'd received the needle-stick injury in his school playground in early August. A second blood test for HIV had shown up negative, confirming that there had been no lasting effect from his fall. Rebecca reported this outcome to Aimee, and looked as if she had something else to add, but then she apparently thought better of it.

The same thing happened several more times over the next two days, until finally Aimee could stand it no longer.

'If there's something you want to talk about, Rebecca,' she told the younger woman in the practice kitchen late on Friday afternoon, 'I'd appreciate it if you'd do so, instead of keeping me in the dark like this.'

'It's not really my business,' Rebecca said slowly. But it was a token protest. It was clear that she considered it very much her business and had quite a bit to say on the subject.

Is it simply a personality clash? Aimee wondered. Rebecca was fiery in spirit, all her moods fully felt and fully expressed. Aimee's temperament was steadier, but in any other situation she could very easily have appreciated and enjoyed Marshall's daughter's passion enormously.

I want so much to be able to like her... Oddly, she'd sensed more than once that Rebecca felt the same.

'Please, make it your business if it will help,' Aimee said to Rebecca carefully now.

'Don't condescend—'

'I'm not!'

'OK, I will say it, then. I want to know why you're going to Marianne Deutschkron's wedding with Dad,' Rebecca muttered forcefully, her eyes ablaze and her wild hair beginning to escape from its colourful clip. 'Why, Aimee? Do you actually enjoy rubbing salt into his wounds? He cares about you. You must know that. What do you gain from stringing him along like this when apparently you don't reciprocate what he feels?'

Rebecca shook her head and seemed close to tears.

'I just don't understand, Aimee,' she went on. 'And I want to ask you, if his well-being means anything to you, please, don't go to that wedding!'

Aimee could hardly speak. She was burning all over at the intensely felt speech from Marshall's daughter, which no one else could have heard. Rebecca had spoken throughout in a very low voice, but that didn't take anything away from the passion in what she'd said.

'I knew,' Aimee managed at last, 'but I hadn't realised your feelings were so strong. Of course I won't go to the wedding.'

'It's not just the wedding,' Rebecca began.

'I realise… I understand…' Aimee cut in clumsily. 'But that's a start, and it's all I can offer you at the moment.'

'I see…'

'No, you don't. You couldn't possibly. But I'm doing my best.'

Not trusting herself to say another word, Aimee fled the kitchen, convinced that the painful exchange had only made everything worse.

Nonetheless, as soon as she reached home about an hour and a half later, she picked up the phone and dialled Marshall's number. Best get this over with. He should be home by now, she hoped, but later on he might disappear for his jog, and she had the idea that he'd been taking rather a long time over it just lately.

He answered on the fourth ring, and she realised at once that she should have prepared her excuse beforehand.

'I'm sorry,' she began immediately. 'I've realised I won't be able to come to the wedding with you tomorrow after all.'

There was a tiny pause, then a thoughtful, 'Ah.'

Another pause followed, longer this time. She could picture him at the other end of the line, standing by the hall table and fingering the stretchy spiral cord of the phone as he spoke, as she'd seen him doing so often at the practice. Perhaps he was cradling the instrument against his shoulder while opening the day's mail, as he often did at work. Or perhaps he was focused on the call more intently, as she was.

'Everything all right, I hope?' he asked at last.

'It's fine,' she said.

'Bonnie, too?'

I could use her as an excuse.

But it wouldn't have been the truth, and she didn't dare take advantage of the darling little girl's precarious progress. Superstitious perhaps, but she'd never forgive herself if Bonnie had a setback. She'd been discharged from hospital last Saturday, and was due here at the flat in half an hour so that Sarah and Jason could paint the nursery and then go out for a meal. It would be the first real break they'd have had together since Bonnie's birth as they'd spent so much time at the hospital and Sarah had had a lot of trouble with learning to express her milk successfully.

'Bonnie's doing well,' she said. 'It's nothing like that, Marsh. I simply realised I shouldn't have said yes. Not when—that is, I wish Mrs Deutschkron's daughter and her fiancé every happiness in the world, but you and I—'

'Does this have anything to do with Rebecca? With something she said?'

Aimee hadn't expected the question, and was already too churned up inside to find a way of avoiding an answer. 'Yes,' she admitted.

'What did she say?'

'Quite a lot, but what it amounted to was right. It's…hard enough, seeing each other at the practice. There's no sense in heaping on the punishment. I've— I really must be firm about it from now on, Marshall. Take Rebecca to the wedding instead.'

She expected him to argue, but he didn't, and they both limped to a stilted end of the conversation.

Marshall stood in the hallway with the phone still in his hand for a good minute after the call, debating his options. He reached a decision by default. He couldn't accept inaction, therefore he could only storm round to Rebecca's and demand to know how and why she'd upset Aimee in the way she obviously had.

Could this be the root of the whole problem? he wondered. Was Aimee afraid of coming between him and Rebecca because of Rebecca's unaccountable dislike of her?

It was only a short drive from his place to Surry Hills, and he found his daughter and her husband in the middle of cooking their evening meal, though he had a strong feeling that they'd already been distracted from their task even before he'd appeared on the scene.

Harry had lipstick smeared on his cheek, and Rebecca's top was caught up at the back. On their stove a pot of water boiled merrily with the lid off and nothing in it at all.

Marshall didn't care what he was interrupting.

'Harry, I'd like to speak to my daughter alone, if you don't mind.'

He didn't make the slightest effort to disguise the ominous resonance to his tone or the flash of intent in his eyes. Some weeks ago, he'd had such a very satisfying image in his mind of himself throwing Aimee across the saddle of his wild black stallion and galloping off with her into the fortress of his medieval castle.

In the absence of stallions and castles of any description, he'd now reached the point where he intended to behave just as masterfully with no appropriate props whatsoever. It might not resolve the situation to his satisfaction, but it would have to at least provide a valve from which some of the emotional steam within him could escape!

'I'm out of here,' Harry agreed cheerfully. He knew his volatile wife rather well, and refused to see the heated appeal in her eyes. 'I think you're in trouble, Rebecca,' he told her. 'But I'm sure you can deal with it! I'll go for a walk.'

He disappeared through the front door less than a minute later, singing a cheerful, tuneless song under his breath. Rebecca cast one final, alarmed look at his retreating form, then gave up on his support and turned to face Marsh, evidently deciding that attack was the best form of defence.

'I don't appreciate being treated like this, Dad,' she began. 'There's nothing we can't talk about in front of—'

'Rebecca!' Marshall was in no mood to have the tables turned on him tonight. He loved his daughter with all his heart, but her pregnancy-heightened feelings weren't on the agenda at the moment.

'I don't know what you said to Aimee today,' he began, leaving her in no doubt that interruptions wouldn't be tolerated. 'I don't know what you've been saying to her…or communicating to her through your crystal clear body language…over the past three months and more. But you're going to start by apologising to her for questioning her acceptance of my invitation to go to Marianne Deutschkron's wedding, and you're going to take it from there.'

'Dad—'

'I'm beginning to suspect very strongly that whatever has gone wrong between Aimee and myself is very largely due to the fact that she's sensitive about your hostility, and somehow I'm going to get you removed from the equation so that I have a fighting chance of winning what I want.' He gave a jerky, forceful sigh. 'Rebecca, I know you care about me. Can't you accept that championing my cause the way you've been doing is only achieving the very thing you've been afraid of on my behalf?'

'Do you really think that's what it is, Dad?' she argued, frowning. 'If it was just that, then surely—'

'I'm not interested in arguing about it, or in theorising about the possibilities, gypsy,' he barked huskily. 'Just go and apologise, and let's at least see if we can get back to square one.'

'If you—'

'Just...*do*...it!' Although he hadn't raised his voice, its power was unmistakable.

She nodded, accepting the strength of his will, and he almost laughed at the struggle she was having to keep back her flow of words. 'Now?' she squeaked at last.

'Now,' he confirmed briskly. 'Harry will have dinner ready for when you get back. I'll tell him what's going on. Here's her address. I've driven past it. It's one of those featureless 1960s red-brick buildings that stick out like a sore thumb in that area. I almost thought I must have got the address wrong at first. But you can't miss it. There should be parking in one of the side streets.'

'You're being very helpful all of a sudden.'

'You've just seen the iron fist, now I've put on the velvet glove, but don't be fooled.'

There was a surprising exhilaration in taking control like this, he found, showing what he felt instead of manfully bottling it up as he'd been struggling to do for months. He suddenly felt as virile as a man of half his age, and as strong as the horse conjured up by his imagination.

'Oh, there's no danger of that!' Rebecca said hastily.

'I'm glad to hear it, because this is a side to my nature

that you may be seeing more of in the future!' he threatened with grim emphasis.

'I'll...look forward to it,' Rebecca replied faintly.

They found Harry leaning on the black iron railing out the front, looking quite relaxed as he enjoyed the mild evening air.

'All fixed up?' he asked.

'I'm being sent on an urgent mission to Aimee,' Rebecca said, her colour still high. She had a rebellious cloud over her features, but when Harry raised his eyebrows she conceded in a jerky tone, 'Dad's right. I haven't meant to, but I've made things worse. Hope I've got the tact to start undoing the damage now.'

'I have every faith in you, dearest,' Harry told her solemnly, then he and Marshall watched as Rebecca climbed into her car, parked in the street, and drove away.

'Everything OK?' Harry asked laconically after she'd gone.

'Remember when I decided to take a helpful hand in your courtship?' Marshall reminded his son-in-law.

'Take it slowly, you told me,' Harry agreed. 'Not the best advice you've ever given, Marsh.'

'No. Quite. I should have stayed well out of the whole thing. Now it's Rebecca's turn to prove that she can do likewise.'

'I can see where my wife gets her spirit from at times like this,' Harry mused, casting his eyes up and down Marshall's form as if he could see the energy that radiated from it. 'Coming in for a drink?'

'*Please!*' Marshall answered his son-in-law fervently.

CHAPTER NINE

WHEN she put down the phone after her conversation with Marshall, Aimee went briskly to her small bedroom to change into a soft, summery knit skirt and T-shirt, and kicked off shoes and pantihose to leave her feet bare.

She'd done the right thing, and she wasn't going to spend the entire evening dwelling on the matter, playing their exchange over and over in her mind. There were other things on her agenda.

The flat was starting to feel like home at last. She'd been here for over a month now, and everything was sorted out. The excess furniture had been disposed of, and all her boxes had been unpacked.

She'd looked at her budget and decided she could afford to splash out a little, giving a lift to the place by adding a tub of flowering annuals to the tiny balcony and two new prints on the walls, both of them landscapes with far more appeal than the view from her windows.

Spending so carefully, it had reminded her of the way she'd stretched her housekeeping money during her marriage, and she'd concluded, I can do this. I'm used to it. I'm doing it for a different reason now, and no one's going to suddenly turn up with a necklace or a new dress or the announcement that we're getting a new lounge suite. There's no safety net, as there used to be, but it's still something I've done before.

She'd even painted the kitchen the previous weekend, with the landlord's permission, choosing four different modern colours to pick out trim and cabinets and handles so that the room looked bright and pretty, with its boxy, cramped proportions somewhat disguised.

William had visited a couple of times. At nineteen, he'd been too caught up in his own concerns to question her about her choice of living space. The name 'Emily' had come up several times, spoken with a sort of misty-eyed reverence, coupled with a gruff and artificial offhandedness that confirmed Aimee's earlier suspicions. William was in love, had hopes of success, but wasn't yet counting his emotional chickens. She felt for him. No wonder he didn't have much time to think about his dear old mum!

However, Aimee knew that Sarah, when she got there in a few minutes, would probably be more critical and questioning about her mother's new home but, like any new parent about to leave her baby for the first time, she would be more concerned with Bonnie than anything else.

And so it proved. Sarah and Jason arrived a little late and very flustered, in the midst of an argument about whose job it had been to feed the cat.

'We forgot the nappy bag and had to go back,' Sarah said. She held a sleeping Bonnie in her arms.

'Where do you want the bassinet?' Jason asked. He had it by the handles, and its wicker creaked as he swung it a little.

'In the bedroom,' Aimee decided.

'Which…?'

'There's only one. The other door is just the linen cupboard,' she told him. 'Put the bassinette on the bed.'

'I didn't realise you'd chosen somewhere so small,' Sarah said.

'It's all I need,' Aimee pointed out crisply. 'I'm planning on spending a fair bit of time at your place!'

'Maybe we shouldn't leave her. We won't paint her room after all,' Sarah suddenly decided.

Aimee had been prepared for this, and had her arguments ready. First, she was a nurse. Second, she was a grandmother, and she'd had babies herself. They weren't a different species. She and Bonnie would be fine, both of them! And help was only a phone call away. It wasn't as if Sarah and Jason were leaving town.

'Ring up on the mobile,' Jason urged. 'Don't hesitate. The moment you need us.'

'It'll be fine!'

At four weeks of age, Bonnie was still mainly on tube feeds of expressed breast milk, as well as the occasional bolus feed via a bottle. She was starting to understand what was required of her when confronted with an actual breast, but wasn't yet taking nearly enough that way to gain weight through the natural approach alone.

In addition, her doctors still felt that larger feeds made the danger of painful and damaging reflux much greater at a time when the site of her surgery had still only just healed. But since Bonnie wasn't taking her milk directly from the breast, there was absolutely no reason why Aimee couldn't manage the set programme of feeds, as well as changing a nappy or two as necessary.

'Now, with the tube—' Sarah began, as Bonnie stirred into semi-wakefulness.

'I know about tubes,' Aimee promised, and after only ten minutes more of anxious parental questions and eager grandmotherly reassurances Sarah and Jason were persuaded on their way. Bonnie, in the bassinet on Aimee's bed, was now happily asleep again.

Three minutes later, there was a knock on the door. Aimee had been more than half expecting it, and she was so sure it would be Sarah and Jason, announcing that they couldn't do it or they'd forgotten to tell her something vital, that she hauled the door open with an indulgent smile on her face and actually gasped at the sight of Rebecca, her cloud of dark hair framing an uneasy expression.

'Is this a bad time?' Rebecca asked eagerly at once, as if she was rather hoping it would be.

'No,' Aimee answered her carefully. 'I was expecting my daughter and son-in-law, that's all. They've left Bonnie with me for the first time, and they were very nervous. I thought they'd rushed back in a fit of remorse.'

Rebecca laughed dutifully on cue, and Aimee thought to herself, Why do I bother? Why do I pretend everything's fine? Why do I try to cajole her into liking me with lame humour? Why do I persist in fighting this losing battle?

'Can I come in?' Rebecca asked, with unusual diffidence.

'Of course.'

She stood aside, and Rebecca stepped into the flat.

There was no entrance hall. The front door opened directly into the living room, where Rebecca looked stranded amidst the still slightly too crowded furnishings.

'I've come to apologise,' she said, before Aimee could come out with an offer of refreshment.

'For what?' she questioned cautiously.

'For questioning your right to accept Dad's invitation to Marianne Deutschkron's wedding.'

'Did he send you?' Aimee asked.

'Yes,' Rebecca admitted at once. 'But don't think that I'm here reluctantly.'

'You look reluctant.'

'That's rather in the nature of apologies, isn't it?' She laughed awkwardly, but there had been a quiet sincerity to her tone. 'No matter how right it is, and how much you want to do it, it's never fun.'

'That's true,' Aimee answered slowly.

'Can we perhaps talk about—?' Rebecca began, then

there came an odd snorting, gagging sound and a cry from the bedroom.

'Bonnie!' Aimee exclaimed, and darted to open the door.

'That didn't sound quite right,' Rebecca said.

'No, it didn't. She's just woken up, obviously, but what was that sound?'

Aimee soon discovered what had happened.

Bonnie had somehow managed to pull out the nasogastric tube through which most of her nutrition now came. It had become untaped from her face and was clutched in her hand, a victim of the grasp reflex, and it was snaking back and forth across Bonnie's tightly screwed-up face as she cried and flapped her tiny arms up and down.

Sarah's precious milk, which should have been trickling drop by drop through the tube and into Bonnie's stomach, driven by a carefully calibrated pump, was covering her in a spray of tiny white droplets.

'I don't know what to do,' Aimee said blankly to Rebecca, trying not to panic.

She picked up the crying baby and began to comfort her, feeling the rush of almost painful tenderness and love which had been a part of her response to Bonnie since her birth.

The baby had filled out a little now, but was still tiny, and her black birth hair had almost disappeared. In the right light, you could just see, with the help of a little wishful thinking, the golden glints of newer, fairer hair growing through. She was utterly precious, and if anything at all went wrong…

With the tube out of the way, however, her crying soon stopped and she was perfectly happy, but Aimee and Rebecca both knew that the problem wasn't over.

'Rebecca, could you get it back in?' Aimee asked anxiously. 'How much of an emergency is this?'

'I could try,' Rebecca said slowly. They'd both forgotten the subject of the interrupted conversation in the face of this more urgent issue. 'But I wouldn't really feel comfortable about it.'

'Then should we take her to the hospital, and get it done there?'

'Best, I think,' Rebecca agreed. 'If there was no other option, I'd do it and there'd probably be no problem, but it can be very tricky after the sort of surgery she's had, and I'm not familiar with all the details of her case. Is she still on any drugs?'

'Yes, a couple to try and deal with her reflux. Something that helps her muscles push the milk through more efficiently and a drug to lower the acidity of her stomach juices so they don't damage the site of her surgery. She's healing well, though, and Jason and Sarah are handling her care at home wonderfully.'

'Do you want to phone them?' Rebecca asked.

Aimee thought for a moment, then decided aloud, 'I won't, I don't think. I would if you weren't here, but they so badly needed this evening. They've been under so much strain for the past few months. They had her room all prepared for painting, too, before heading out to dinner. They'd shifted the furniture and put down drop sheets and taped the trim. If they don't get it done tonight… But that's not really the issue, of course. I feel if I phone them in a panic now, they'll decide that it's wrong of them to try to get time to themselves, and with all the extra care that Bonnie needs…'

'I know what you mean,' Rebecca soothed. 'You don't want any of the four of you to fall at the first hurdle. We'll be fine. It really isn't an emergency, just a nuisance. I'll come with you and see you safely through it all, and I'm tempted to tell you not to even say anything about it to them, except that I know they wouldn't thank you for that.'

'No, they wouldn't,' Aimee agreed. 'All right, we won't ring them. I have a baby capsule fitted in my car. We'll drive straight to Southshore. Thanks, Rebecca.'

'I'll just phone Harry and tell him not to expect me for a while.'

Rebecca took a mobile phone out of her bag and made the call, not troubling to hide the teasing tenderness in her voice as she spoke to her husband. Putting the little instrument away a few moments later, she looked at Aimee. 'Ready?'

Bonnie was happy to be in the car and went straight back to sleep. Aimee had to talk herself out of an absurd fear that the weight would simply start falling off her fragile body during this enforced absence of feeding. What if the accident and emergency department was crowded? What if they had to wait for hours? Beside her in the passenger seat, Rebecca didn't need her to explain her tension, and was alert to how distracted she was as well.

'Watch out for that red car up ahead,' she warned at one point. 'It's changed lanes twice now without indicating.'

'Thanks,' Aimee said for the second time in just a few minutes.

'Please, don't keep saying that,' Rebecca answered, and they were both thinking about all the conflict between them over the past few months. There was a silence, in which Rebecca shifted several times. It could simply have been the increasing discomfort of her pregnancy—Aimee's car was by no means roomy—but she knew it wasn't.

Finally, Rebecca said, 'I've left you in no doubt how I feel about the problems between you and Dad, have I, Aimee?'

'No, no doubt at all,' she agreed, reluctant to break the

strange peace that had grown between them because of their shared concern over Bonnie.

'You don't seem like the sort of person who'd deliberately use him, or trample over his feelings.'

'I— Well, no, I'm not.'

'Yet you know how hurt he is. I'm not accusing or attacking. I just don't understand. I know I'm overprotective—'

'Is that all it is? You seem to dislike me so very strongly.'

'Not at all! But Dad has no one but me. Simon is on the other side of the world. Dad has friends, but they're not people he confides in. He was brought up to be reserved about his personal life. Even to me. I'm not ashamed to say I'll champion his cause to the point of coming across as a complete shrew—just talk to me, Aimee!' she interrupted herself passionately. 'Tell me why you threw my father's care for you back in his face!'

'Because it wouldn't have been fair to do anything else,' Aimee said.

'To whom? To him?'

'To him. To you and your brother. To myself.'

She turned into the hospital entrance, relieved that they'd almost arrived. Another minute of Rebecca's determined probing would have her dangerously close to telling the whole story of her changed circumstances, which she remained determined not to do.

'I'll pull into the bay beside the A and E entrance,' she told Rebecca. 'We'll get Bonnie out of the car, then I'll go and park while you take her in, if that's all right.'

'It's fine. But I don't—'

'I have reasons, Rebecca, for what I've done,' she said firmly. 'I didn't do it lightly. But it's private. And it's hurt me…been as hard for me as it's been for your father. Please, can we say no more about it?'

The accident and emergency department was fairly busy, but not yet filled with the inevitable Friday late night crew of cases related to alcohol and drug abuse. The triage nurse on duty placed Bonnie near the head of the queue, and she was soon taken into a cubicle where another nurse reinserted the tube.

Although it took only a minute or two, it was painful to watch, and Aimee had tears in her eyes by the time the tube was in place. Bonnie struggled and gagged, brought up saliva and had to be suctioned—Rebecca stepped into assist with this—and she went on crying even once the job was done and the tape was in place.

That tape! It was irritating her sensitive new skin, making it red and rough. It made her look like a child who'd been ill, and added to her aura of fragility.

And the thing wasn't over. Next, Bonnie had to be wheeled off to X-Ray to check that the tube was positioned correctly in order to avoid any risk of the end of it irritating the sites of her surgery.

'Bad news,' the nurse reported when she returned from X-ray. 'Not quite right this time—I'm sorry.'

She repositioned it, which wasn't quite as stressful for Bonnie as getting it down in the first place, but it came close. When Rebecca and Aimee were finally able to take Bonnie back to the car, they were both tense and drained by the whole thing.

'She doesn't seem to like the tube, does she?' Aimee said.

'Most babies don't like tubes, especially as they start to get older and more aware,' Rebecca answered. 'Have Sarah and Jason been given an estimate on when it can go?'

'I don't think so. I suppose it depends on her weight gain, and how well she learns to suck.'

'Those things, and how much she's affected by the reflux,' Rebecca agreed. 'A big feed all at once is going to come back up more readily than the slow, continuous feeds she gets through the pump and tube.'

Aimee felt her eyes tearing yet again. 'It's so hard,' she said. 'I never had to go through anything like this with a baby. They're both handling it so well and, as for Bonnie, she's already a heroine…'

Bonnie fell asleep in the car almost at once, tired out by crying, and when they reached Summer Hill the two women each took one side of the baby capsule's handle and carefully carried her upstairs without waking her. There was a degree of silent co-operation between the two of them that hadn't been there before, and it was like a soothing balm to Aimee's soul. She didn't dare to think beyond the simple hope that it might make things easier at the practice, however.

Once upstairs, she said quietly to Rebecca, 'We'll leave her in the capsule, shall we? On my bed? She looks so peaceful I don't want to move her to the bassinet.'

'I'll help you reattach and set the pump.'

'Jason wrote it all down for me. Thanks enormously for coming to the hospital.'

'It was no problem, Aimee,' Rebecca said, and again there was a sense of peace and trust and respect between them.

It was cramped in Aimee's bedroom as they settled Bonnie on the bed and reattached and set the pump. The milk began to snake its way through the tube. While Aimee was still watching its progress rather anxiously, she stepped to one side without looking and knocked Rebecca, who was bending a little to watch Bonnie, sharply in the cheek with her elbow.

'Oh, lord, I'm so sorry!'

Rebecca had straightened and was pressing a palm to her cheek where it obviously hurt.

'No problem,' she managed, then blurted out rather too frankly, 'There isn't room to swing a cat in here. Why didn't you get a bigger place?'

Like Rebecca, Aimee was too tired and distracted to think before she spoke. 'Yes. Nice if I could have afforded it,' she said bluntly.

Before Rebecca could say anything in reply to this, the phone rang and it was Sarah, her tone high and impatient and worried.

'This is the fourth time I've phoned, Mum, and you haven't picked up. We've been frantic.'

Aimee told the story, and had to summon a truckload of diplomacy and maternal wisdom to argue Sarah and Jason out of abandoning their plan to eat out, now that they'd finished painting Bonnie's bedroom walls, and coming straight over to take their baby home.

Sarah finally conceded. 'She's been looking like she might do it at any time, the way she flaps her arms and grips anything that gets into her little fists. I know it's not your fault, Mum, but I feel terrible for her that I wasn't there when it happened. Oh, hell, I'm going all shaky.'

'Go out to dinner,' Aimee soothed. 'She's fast asleep now, and the feed is going in as it should. I know you wanted to get her room done, and you have, but that wasn't the only priority and now you need the break!'

In the background, Rebecca signalled to Aimee that she was about to leave. She'd been standing patiently during this conversation, trying not to listen. That, of course, was impossible in this one-bedroom flat, and Rebecca in the best of circumstances would have seemed too radiant and energetic for the place, like a tropical bird trapped in a cruelly small cage.

Over the past few minutes she'd been prowling, looking out at the uninspiring view from the window, bumping awkwardly into the heavy couch as she stepped back to admire one of Aimee's new prints.

Acknowledging the younger woman's signals, Aimee mouthed, 'Thanks!' Then she watched Rebecca leave, a thoughtful expression apparent on her vibrantly pretty face, surrounded by her mass of hair.

It was almost half past eight, and suddenly the flat was silent. Aimee realised that she was hungry. Knowing that the baby might wake at any time, she made herself a quick cheese and ham omelette and ate it with fingers of buttered toast, a tiny salad scarcely worthy of the name and a cup of tea.

Then she tiptoed into the bedroom and spent fifteen minutes simply gazing with unashamed love at tiny Bonnie Louise, letting her thoughts drift at will until they suddenly snagged against the realization that she had no idea, as things stood, whether she was going to Marianne Deutschkron's wedding with Marshall the next afternoon or not.

Marshall himself wasn't in a similar state of doubt, apparently. He phoned her at nine the next morning, and there was something about his voice and manner—a combination of authority and confidently expressed tenderness—which she hadn't heard since the beginning of August.

'I'm so glad you're coming after all, Aimee.'

'Yes, I…I'm glad, too.'

'Rebecca told me about Bonnie pulling out her tube last night.'

'Oh, it was awful. It was good to have Rebecca there. I've already thanked her for staying, and for coming to the hospital with me, of course, but when you next speak to her—'

'She doesn't need any more thanks,' he said firmly. 'It was the least she could have done. We had a good talk last night.'

'Did you?' she answered automatically.

He'd given a weight to the statement which suggested that his talk with Rebecca had been important, but Aimee couldn't imagine why. It would be nice if the hostility between herself and Marshall's daughter had finally been ironed out, but it didn't make a big difference to the state of their own relationship.

'I'll pick you up at two-twenty, shall I?' he went on. 'The wedding is at Seaforth House, in Randwick, at three.'

'I'll be ready.'

She was. Ready, and nervous, and aware that her dress looked like the six-year-old model it was. Not badly dated in style, as its silhouette was classic and clinging, but not quite the right length and not as crisp and fresh in its colours as it could have been, after numerous launderings.

A new one had not only been ill advised from a budgetary point of view, but had also been something she knew she would regret on a more personal level. Just as, when Marshall appeared at her door, she was already regretting that she'd agreed to go at all.

He looked impossibly distinguised in his charcoal-grey suit, with its crisp white shirt beneath an understated silk tie in a subtle print. The shade of maroon in the silk exactly matched the maroon in her dress, and they would have looked like quite a stylish couple if they'd been a couple at all.

He almost behaved as if they were a couple today, and

it disturbed her. Although he didn't kiss her at her door, didn't touch her at all, there was an unmistakable heat to his regard and a potent and deliberate aura of sensual virility to the set of his body. He didn't have to tell her, in some perfunctory way, that she looked good. His opinion on the matter was written all over his face, and he didn't seem to care in the least about this openness.

What had happened to him in twenty-four hours?

'Let's go…'

'Yes, there's no need to ask you in, is there?' Aimee said as she closed the door behind her, hearing the breathlessness in her voice and knowing he'd heard it, too.

He didn't answer, just gave a tiny nod and stood back to let her lead the way down the breeze-filled open concrete stairway. She felt his hand very lightly in the middle of her back, but it didn't linger there, and she had to fight the need to turn to him and invite a greater intimacy of touch. Was he doing it deliberately? It felt that way.

They didn't talk much during the half-hour drive. He seemed content to make the occasional observation about neutral things. The traffic. The weather. She wasn't sure why she had such a strong sense that he was biding his time, or what the source of the potent new confidence in him was, but she felt that the ground beneath her feet was, metaphorically, as unstable as a fault line in an earthquake-prone landscape.

She almost blurted out something agitated and edgy about boundaries, limits they'd set, respect for her decision, but since he'd actually said and done nothing to challenge what she'd told him about their relationship three months before, she didn't know how to begin and held her tongue.

The wedding was everything Hilde Deutschkron had been hoping for to crown her last months of life. Seaforth House was a gracious old mansion, recently renovated and converted into an elegant function centre, complete with lush and perfectly manicured grounds where the 150 guests were free to wander.

The ceremony, conducted by a civil marriage celebrant, was romantic and carefully thought out, a mixture of traditional vows and classic poetry spoken by the celebrant and the bride and groom, and wonderful singing by a friend of the bride.

Marianne looked gorgeous in an ankle-length ivory silk dress, cut with simple flair. She carried red roses that matched the crimson taffeta of the two bridesmaids' dresses, and her dark hair was swept up into a Grecian knot at the back of her head. Jonathan was clearly wondering how he'd been lucky enough to find such a bride, and Hilde smiled like a beam of pure sunshine all through the ceremony, while tears raced each other down her cheeks, hopelessly blotting her make-up.

Aimee cried, too, and Marshall teased her about it in a murmur as the ceremony came to an end. 'Is it genetic or something?'

'Absolutely,' she sniffed in reply, grinning. 'You should have seen me at Sarah's and Jason's wedding. Honestly, you can't imagine how satisfying it feels. It's one of the best things about being female, that I'm allowed—'

'Expected, even?' he suggested.

'Expected,' she agreed, 'to cry at weddings.'

'Will I have to escort you outside to recover? There's a break for us guests while the principals submit to ritual photography.'

'I'll recover in the powder room first,' she said. 'Then, please, do escort me outside. I'd love to see those wonderful gardens.'

There was an unconsciously wistful note to her voice. She missed the garden at Woollahra.

Marshall was waiting for her at the glass-panelled side door when she emerged, her eye make-up fully repaired. Hilde Deutschkron was still at work before the mirror, holding the professional wedding photographer at bay until she was presentable.

The two women had laughed at themselves, and Hilde had been so overwrought that Aimee had had to help her open her pill bottle to extract the dose of painkiller she was due for. She was already looking very tired, and would have to use a wheelchair soon in order to get through the long afternoon and evening. Aimee guessed that her condition would deteriorate rapidly after today, which had provided Hilde's reason for fighting for life since August.

'I'm still intrigued by the phenomenon of your tears,' Marshall said as they went down the slate steps and along a gravel path edged by roses in full bloom.

'Don't get me started again!' Aimee laughed, trying to ignore how emotional she still felt. It could just be Marianne and Jonathan, of course. Or Hilde. It really had nothing to do with Marsh.

'I won't,' he promised. 'But tell me if I've got it right. Is it the solemnity of it? The weight of the public commitment they're making? The holiness?'

'All that,' she agreed. 'And the beauty of it. The love that goes with it. The innocence of their courage.'

'You're wondering if they really understand what "for worse" can mean?' he suggested quietly.

'Yes.'

'Far better to face the worst together, though, isn't it, Aimee?' he said in a low voice that trembled with meaning.

They'd reached the most secluded corner of the garden, a stone-paved area, slightly sunken, where there was a white wrought-iron table and several matching chairs, screened from the house and the rest of the garden by a thick bank of grass green agapanthus plants, their tall flower stalks budding with bluish-purple flowers but not yet in full bloom.

'Not always,' she answered him. 'By no means always, Marsh.'

He moved closer to her and took her hands in his, and sudden understanding lit up like a flash of lightning inside her. Two things she was now sure of. Firstly, that he'd brought her to this spot quite deliberately because of its privacy. Secondly, that he now knew—or had guessed—a good part of why she'd turned her back on what they could have had three months ago.

'I think you're wrong,' he said.

His fingers slid up her arms, brushstrokes of sensation all along the sensitive skin. He was looking down into her eyes, his face serious and searching, strong and confident, all at the same time.

'You don't know,' she protested feebly. 'You can't.'

'No, I don't,' he agreed. 'Not all of it. But it's to do with money, isn't it? Your financial situation?'

'It's not something I—'

'Everything was going fine,' he went on, ignoring her attempt to block him.

She could have struggled out of his arms, but knew somehow that it wouldn't have been enough. He would have come after her, held her again, demanded answers, challenged her with searching and perceptive questions. Nothing was going to fob him off today.

'Going fine,' he repeated. 'What we both felt was so strong and good, and then you had some news. I could sense it right from that Saturday after we'd slept together when you phoned me and cancelled my idea of meeting again that weekend.

'You were like some creature that had been dealt a blow. You turned in on yourself. Yes, I could sense it, but I thought that you'd eventually tell me what had happened and I'd be there to help. I thought it was Sarah and the baby at first. Then you ended it completely, and that hurt so much that I couldn't think straight for a while.'

'Oh, Marsh…!'

'A long while! Tell me, Aimee! You owed money, you'd got deeply into debt somehow. You had to sell your home. Rebecca told me that your new flat, attractive though you've made it, isn't exactly generous in proportions.'

'No, it is rather small.' That was as much as she dared to concede.

'But why on earth did you think it mattered?' Marshall said, betraying a degree of helplessness for the first time. 'It doesn't matter. I'm simply not going to allow such a stupid, venal commodity as money to interfere for one second longer with what we have, and if that's as bad as the "for worse" is that you'll be thinking of when we get married and make those vows to each other in front of those we love, then…then…'

His fluency deserted him finally and he groaned as he abandoned inadequate language and pulled her face towards him with impatient hands. Aimee gasped as his mouth met hers. She tried to turn away but he wouldn't let her. The touch of his lips was hot and urgent and imperious, and she couldn't help responding with a passion just as strong.

The fabric of their clothing swished together and she felt the hardness of his thighs through the silk around her own legs. His arms enclosed her and his hands moulded the shape of her back then caressed the curve of her behind, making the fabric slip higher.

He lifted her off the ground, covering her face with kisses and swinging her around, disorientating her and throwing her off balance so that when he put her down again at last she had to cling to him.

'Marry you? I can't marry you!' she moaned shakily at last.

'You can, and you will, unless you can tell me that there's something else in the way, Aimee! Is there something else?'

'No. Yes! It's not "only" money. It's…it's… Oh, this is hopeless!'

'It isn't,' he said, and his sudden calm was like a shelf of dry rock in a heaving sea. 'On the contrary. It's actually full of hope, that we're talking about it, and that I'm getting a chance, at last, to shoot down in flames anything you can throw at me. Take your time, Aimee, and talk, please! We'll walk if you want to. Leave, even. They'll hardly miss us.'

'I don't want to leave. Or walk. This spot is—'

'Private,' he agreed, reading her thoughts.

He seized a chair and spun it so that the edge of its seat nudged the back of her legs. She sat down, then he pulled one up for himself and sat facing her, pressing his knees against hers and taking both her hands so that she had no choice but to look into his eyes and…

'Talk!' Marshall commanded again, his thumbs making an acutely sensitive exploration of her hands and fingers.

'I'm broke, Marshall.'

'So I'm beginning to understand.'

'But I'm not in any real debt.' Aimee lifted her chin and gleaned some pride from that. She was paying off those awful credit-card bills a little more each payday. 'The house was never in my name. The children don't know that. They don't realise what's happened…'

She explained every one of the secrets she'd been keeping, protecting Peter, protecting Sarah and Thomas and William. 'And Rebecca and Simon, too,' she finished.

He looked completely astonished. Horrified. 'What on earth does this have to do with them?'

'Your inheritance,' she answered.

'My—'

'It's common knowledge around the practice. You can't ask people like Bev and Chrissie not to talk. It's well meant. The money from your father-in-law. I've known all along how Rebecca felt, how she distrusted me. How much worse would it have been if she'd had to see me walk into marriage with you and a huge share of the money her grandfather left which is supposed to go to her and Simon? I'm not a gold-digger.'

'Oh, lord, of course you're not!'

'But, more than that, far more, I was dependent on Alan during the whole of our marriage, you see. And it's just not a position I want to be in again.'

She sketched some graphic examples, then went on, 'I couldn't do it. For all our sakes.'

'Oh, Aimee!' he rasped painfully, 'And you've kept all this to yourself?'

'What else could I have done?' she demanded, her voice high. 'To talk about it would only have been to open myself up to blandishments from all sides. Sarah and the boys would have wanted to give me the money from the house, and they need it more than I do. Particularly Sarah. She couldn't go back to work and leave fragile little Bonnie with a stranger for the sake of something as soulless as a mortgage. You would have argued. You're going to argue, aren't you? See!' She shook her head and her hands frantically. 'Even now...'

'I'm not going to argue,' he said quietly. 'At least, not yet. Not before I present you with some facts.'

'Facts? What can facts—?'

'These facts,' he answered firmly. 'Firstly, that the money I inherited from Joy's father has already been made over entirely to Rebecca and Simon. I never had any intention of keeping it for myself. Secondly, that Rebecca's hostility to you had nothing whatever to do with any concern on her part about you usurping her rightful inheritance. I apologise for my daughter's misplaced passion...' he gave a wry smile that made the fine skin at the corners of his eyes fan into the lines of experience she loved '...but it comes from the best of intentions. She cares about me, and all she was afraid of was that you'd hurt me, which you did. You have.' His voice threatened to break. 'So much.'

'Not more than I've hurt myself,' Aimee whispered. 'Never think that.'

This was too painful. She could see the certainty about their future together that burned in him, without yet being able to believe that he could be right.

He was silent for a long moment. 'Is it Alan's ghost that I'm fighting?' he said finally. 'Alan's legacy? Were you very unhappy with him?'

'No,' she answered decisively. 'Not unhappy. Just never...' she searched for words '...credited with being fully an adult. He was a man of his parents' generation in many ways, and his parents were strict, set in their views and their ways. He meant well. He cared for me, and I cared for him.'

'Then can Alan be left out of this?' Marshall asked. 'Tell me, have you ever seen me treat you as less than an adult? And do you still have something to prove to yourself about it? You certainly don't have anything to prove to me! Look at the way you've handled the changes life has thrown at you over these past few months. The way you've set up a new life for yourself in that little flat. The way you responded to Sarah's need. I want as much as you do to approach our marriage—'

He broke off at her restive, protesting movement. 'Our marriage, Aimee,' he insisted, his hands kneading and caressing hers. 'If this was a dream or, no, if this was six months ago,' he corrected himself, 'before any of these issues arose, isn't it what you'd have wanted?'

'Yes,' she admitted. 'Oh, yes, Marshall!'

'And I want us to approach it as equals as much as you do, but when I count up everything we'd be bringing to it, money is the very last thing on my mind, and if I'd known what was getting in our way, we could have had this conversation three months ago and saved ourselves all of this hurt and doubt! Will you marry me, Aimee Hilliard?'

His gaze bored into hers and she could sense his impatience, his force of will and need, and also the tiny steel-hard thread of fear in him, still, that all his reassurance and passion hadn't been enough. For one last moment, she wondered the same thing. Perhaps it hadn't been.

Then she thought about what he'd just said—and had her answer at last.

'Don't wish back the time we've just lost,' she told him heatedly. 'Don't! I needed it. I needed the bad news, and the changes, and the task of handling it on my own. Because now, at last, it means I *can* say yes to you, my dear, dear love. I'm stronger than I was then. I've proved something to myself. I have more to give now, and there's nothing I want more than to give it to you.'

'Then give it to me now, please,' he whispered urgently against her ear, 'because I can't wait for it any longer! Say yes—please!'

'Yes, oh, yes, Marsh, with all my heart!'

EPILOGUE

'REMIND me once more what it is about women and weddings,' Marshall commanded his new bride softly as he slid his lips reluctantly from Aimee's and they both turned to face the modest group of family and friends who'd been invited to witness the simple ceremony.

He could count at least three streaming female faces among the smiles that met his gaze.

There was Rebecca, standing beside a grinning Harry, who was holding their three-month-old baby boy, Jack. There was Sarah, also holding her child, a bouncing Bonnie who was now eight months old, growing fast and rid of all external signs of the problems that had clouded her birth and early weeks. She still suffered from reflux, but was feeding completely from the breast and just starting to express a rather late interest in solids. Beside Sarah, Jason looked both happy and embarrassed at his wife's display of feeling.

Then there was practice partner Grace Gaines, her arm linked through her husband Marcus's. Despite Grace's tears, they looked as if they were reliving their own wedding day, both their faces aglow. Their little Hannah Margaret, who was just two weeks old, was asleep in a baby sling around Marcus's chest and shoulder.

Marshall's son Simon and his girlfriend Julianne had flown from the United States for this occasion, and even Julianne was suspiciously moist around the eyes.

'What is it about men and weddings, I wonder!' Aimee teased him back. 'I can see three happily married husbands with their fingers pulling at their shirt collars as if their necks have increased in size quite dramatically over the course of the past hour. What's that about?'

'Only three happily married husbands?' Marshall queried, running his own finger around the inside of his collar as he spoke.

'And one newly-wed,' Aimee amended. 'Too soon to say if he's happily married or not.'

'Oh, he's happy,' Marshall whispered. 'He's practically bursting with it. That's what accounts for the lump in his throat, you see. And the lump in the throat makes the shirt collar feel tight, and the finger's an attempt to loosen it. So simple. Whereas the tears…'

'Not simple, perhaps,' she agreed, 'but every bit as real.'

Everyone was moving forward now with congratulations on their lips and hugs at the ready. The June day was turning golden as the sun began its descent behind the trees of Marshall's and Aimee's new garden. The early winter weather had been kind to them, providing both sunshine and just the gentle hint of an ocean breeze.

The ocean was just a few hundred metres away, forming a panoramic backdrop to this outdoor ceremony and to the newly renovated house, which was the reason they'd waited over seven months to make their vows to each other.

Marshall had retired from his Sydney practice, and together they'd chosen the little town of Milperra, on the coast a few hours south of Sydney, as their new home. The place hadn't had a doctor in residence for ten years so they'd had to start afresh. They'd found a large, old-fashioned house which they'd divided into two self-contained sections—one for the practice and one for their home.

It had been hard work. Lots of decisions, lots of poring over plans. Most of the work had been done by professional builders, but they'd made the finishing touches and worked on the garden themselves, and would open for business when they returned from their honeymoon in two weeks' time.

Since it would only be a one-doctor practice, Aimee would act as both practice nurse and receptionist, and she'd had to brush up her skills in the latter area. Milperra attracted retired people from Sydney and Canberra, as well as younger people interested in a slower lifestyle, and they'd already received numerous interested enquiries about when they'd be taking on patients.

Marshall's big house in Sydney had been sold, and the changes and decisions they'd made together had already set up a strong foundation of equality in their relationship, taking away Aimee's last lingering doubts about the twin issues of money and independence.

Rebecca was the first to reach the newly-weds, with tears still sparkling in her eyes and a smile almost as wide as the Pacific Ocean lighting up her face. 'I'm so thrilled and happy for you both,' she whispered to Aimee as they held each other in a warm embrace. 'I've never seen Dad look so happy. Thank you for lighting that glow inside him, Aimee.'

Then she turned to her father to hug him even harder, and it was Sarah's turn to hug her mother.

'You look wonderful, Mum,' she said, enfolding her with enthusiastic arms. 'And you spoke so clearly and steadily. Do you remember how I fluffed my lines?'

'How could I forget when you obsessed about it for at least a month afterwards?' Aimee teased.

'Seriously, though...'

'Seriously, I'm too happy and too certain about this to be nervous.'

'I know, and I'm so proud of you, Mum. You deserve

this, and I'm getting a sister at last, and a whole family of doctor in-laws, and a playmate for Bonnie when Rebecca's baby is older.' She dabbed at her eyes once more, and Marshall and Aimee shared a private smile.

A few moments later he drew her aside, under cover of the happy chatter that had begun. Sarah was introducing herself to Julianne. Grace and Marcus were talking to Jason about Bonnie. Simon and William seemed to have a lot in common—including a marked similarity in appearance between Simon's Julianne and William's Emily—and Harry and Thomas were apparently enthusing to each other about snakes.

'You implied to me more than once,' Marshall reminded Aimee softly, 'that one of the impossible things about love at our age was the number of people whose needs had to be considered. Well, they're all here today, and by the looks of them we could have done this for their sakes alone.'

She laughed and conceded his point with a nod. 'We could. We didn't, though,' she said. 'In the end, after all my doubts, we did it for *us*, and that was all the reason I needed.'

Marshall didn't trouble to express his agreement in words. Instead, he said it with the light of love in his eyes, and with his kiss, the first of many, as man and wife, in years to come.